Princess in the Spotlight

Books by

MEG CABOT

THE PRINCESS DIARIES

THE PRINCESS DIARIES, VOLUME II:
PRINCESS IN THE SPOTLIGHT

MEG CABOT

The Princess Diaries, Volume II

Princess in the Spotlight

HARPERCOLLINS*PUBLISHERS*

Typography by Alison Donalty
12 13 14 15

For my grandparents,
Bruce and Patsy Mounsey,
who are nothing like any of the grandparents in this book.

ACKNOWLEDGMENTS

Many thanks to Barb Cabot, Debra Martin Chase, Bill Contardi, Sarah Davies, Laura Langlie, Abby McAden, Alison Donalty, and the usual suspects: Beth Ader, Jennifer Brown, Dave Walton, and especially, Benjamin Egnatz.

Princess in the Spotlight

When things are horrible—just horrible—
I think as hard as ever I can of being a princess.
I say to myself,
"I am a princess."
You don't know how it makes you forget.

A LITTLE PRINCESS
Frances Hodgson Burnett

Okay. So I was just in the kitchen, eating cereal, you know, the usual Monday morning routine, when my mom comes out of the bathroom with this funny look on her face. I mean, she was all pale and her hair was kind of sticking out and she had on her terry cloth robe instead of her kimono, which usually means she's premenstrual.

So I said, "Mom, you want some Midol? Because, no offense, you look like you could use some."

Which is sort of a dangerous thing to say to a premenstrual woman, but you know, she's my mom, and all. It's not like she was going to karate chop me, the way she would if anybody else said that to her.

But she just said, "No. No, thanks," in this dazed voice.

So then I assumed something really horrible had happened. You know, like Fat Louie had eaten another sock, or they were cutting off our electricity again because I'd forgotten to fish the bill out of the salad bowl where Mom keeps stuffing them.

So I grabbed her and I was like, "Mom? Mom, what is it? What's wrong?"

She sort of shook her head, like she does when she's confused over the microwave instructions on a frozen pizza. "Mia," she said, in this shocked but happy way, "Mia. I'm pregnant."

Oh, my God. OH, MY GOD.

My mom is having my Algebra teacher's baby.

I am really trying to take this calmly, you know? Because there isn't any point in getting upset about it.

But how can I *NOT* be upset? My mother is about to become a single parent. *AGAIN.*

You would think she'd have learned a lesson with me and all, but apparently not.

As if I don't have enough problems. As if my life isn't over already. I just don't see how much more I can be expected to take. I mean, apparently, it is not enough that

1. I am the tallest girl in the freshman class.
2. I am also the least endowed in the chest area.
3. Last month, I found out my mother has been dating my Algebra teacher.
4. Also last month, I found out that I am the sole heir to the throne of a small European country.
5. I have to take princess lessons from my paternal grandmother. *Every day.*
6. In December, I am supposed to be introduced to my new countrymen and women on national television (in Genovia, population 50,000, but still).
7. I don't have a boyfriend.

Oh, no. You see, all of that isn't enough of a burden, apparently. Now my mother has to get pregnant out of wedlock. *AGAIN.*

Thanks, Mom. Thanks a whole lot.

And what *about* that? Why weren't she and Mr. Gianini using birth control? Could someone please explain that to me? Whatever happened to her diaphragm? I know she has one. I found it once in the shower when I was a little kid. I took it and used it as a birdbath for my Barbie townhouse for a few weeks, until my mom finally found out and took it away.

And what about condoms??? Do people my mother's age think they are immune to sexually transmitted diseases? They are obviously not immune to pregnancy, so what gives?

This is *so* like my mother. She can't even remember to buy toilet paper. How is she going to remember to use birth control????????

I can't believe this. I really can't believe this.

She hasn't told him. My mother is having my Algebra teacher's baby, *and she hasn't even told him.*

I can tell she hasn't told him, because when I walked in this morning, all Mr. Gianini said was, "Oh, hi, Mia. How are you doing?"

Oh, hi, Mia. How are you doing?????

That is not what you say to someone whose mother is having your baby. You say something like, "Excuse me, Mia, may I see you a moment?"

Then you take the daughter of the woman with whom you have committed this heinous indiscretion out into the hallway, where you fall on bended knee to grovel and beg for her approval and forgiveness. That is what you do.

I can't help staring at Mr. G and wondering what my new baby brother or sister is going to look like. My mom is totally hot, like Carmen Sandiego, only without the trench coat—further proof that I am a biological anomaly, since I inherited neither my mother's thick curly black mane of hair nor her C cup. So there's nothing to worry about there.

But Mr. G, I just don't know. Not that Mr. G isn't good-looking, I guess. I mean, he's tall and has all his hair (score one for Mr. G, since my dad's as bald as a parking meter). But what is with his nostrils? I totally can't figure it out. They are just so . . . big.

I sincerely hope the kid gets my mom's nostrils and Mr. G's ability to divide fractions in his head.

The sad thing is, Mr. Gianini doesn't have the slightest

idea what is about to befall him. I would feel sorry for him if it weren't for the fact that it is all his fault. I know it takes two to tango, but please, my mother is a painter. He is an Algebra teacher.

You tell me who is supposed to be the responsible one.

Monday, October 20, English

Great. Just great.

As if things aren't bad enough, now our English teacher says we have to complete a *journal* this semester. I am not kidding. A *journal*. Like I don't already keep one.

And get this: At the end of every week, we're supposed to *turn our journals in*. For Mrs. Spears to *read*. Because she wants to get to know us. We are supposed to begin by introducing ourselves, and listing our pertinent stats. Later, we are supposed to move on to recording our innermost thoughts and emotions.

She has got to be joking. Like I am going to allow Mrs. Spears to be privy to my innermost thoughts and emotions. I won't even tell my innermost thoughts and emotions to my *mother*. Would I tell them to my *English teacher*?

And I can't possibly turn *this* journal in. There's all sorts of stuff in here I don't want anyone to know. Like how my mother is pregnant by my Algebra teacher, for instance.

Well, I will just have to start a new journal. A *fake* journal. Instead of recording my innermost emotions and feelings in it, I'll just write a bunch of lies, and hand that in instead.

I am such an accomplished liar, I very highly doubt Mrs. Spears will know the difference.

ENGLISH JOURNAL
by Mia Thermopolis

KEEP OUT!!!
THIS MEANS YOU,
UNLESS YOU ARE MRS. SPEARS!!!!!!

An Introduction

NAME:

Amelia Mignonette Grimaldi Thermopolis Renaldo
Known as Mia for short.
Her Royal Highness the princess of Genovia or just
Princess Mia in some circles.

AGE:

Fourteen

YR IN SCHOOL:

Freshman

SEX:

Haven't had it yet. Ha, ha, just kidding, Mrs. Spears!
Ostensibly female, but lack of breast size lends disturbing androgyny.

DESCRIPTION:

Five foot nine
Short mouse-brown hair (new blond highlights)
Gray eyes
Size ten shoe
The rest is not worth remarking on.

PARENTS:

Mother: Helen Thermopolis

OCCUPATION:

Painter

FATHER:

Artur Christoff Phillipe Gerard Grimaldi Renaldo

OCCUPATION:

Prince of Genovia

PARENTS' MARITAL STATUS:

Because I am the result of a fling my mother and father had in college, they never married (each other) and are both currently single. It is probably better this way, since all they ever do is fight.

With each other, I mean.

PETS:

One cat, Fat Louie. Orange and white, Louie weighs twenty-five pounds. Louie is eight years old, and has been on a diet for approximately six of those years. When Louie is upset with us for, say, forgetting to feed him, he eats any socks he might find lying around. Also, he is attracted to small glittery things, and has quite a collection of beer bottle caps and tweezers which he thinks I don't know about, hidden behind the toilet in my bathroom.

BEST FRIEND:

My best friend is Lilly Moscovitz. Lilly has been my best friend since kindergarten. She is fun to hang out with because she is very very smart and has her own public access television show, *Lilly Tells It Like It Is.* She is always thinking up fun things to do, like steal the foamboard sculpture of the Parthenon that the Greek and Latin Derivatives class made for Parents'

Night and hold it for a ransom of ten pounds of lime Starbursts.

Not that that was us, Mrs. Spears. I am just using that as an example of the type of crazy thing Lilly *might* do.

BOYFRIEND:

Ha! I wish.

ADDRESS:

I have lived all of my life in New York City with my mother, except for summers, which I have traditionally spent with my father at his mother's chateau in France. My father's primary residence is Genovia, a small country in Europe located on the Mediterranean between the Italian and French border. For a long time I was led to believe that my father was an important politician in Genovia, like the mayor, or something. Nobody told me that he was actually a member of the Genovian royal family—that he was, in fact, the reigning monarch, Genovia being a principality. I guess nobody ever would have told me, either, if my dad hadn't gotten testicular cancer and become sterile, making me, his illegitimate daughter, the only heir he'll ever have to his throne. Ever since he finally let me in on this *slightly* important little secret (a month ago) Dad has been living at the Plaza Hotel here in New York, while his mother, my grandmère, the dowager princess, teaches me what I need to know in order to be his heir.

For which I can only say: Thanks. Thanks a *whole* lot.

And do you want to know what the *really* sad part is? None of that was lies.

Okay, Lilly knows.

All right, maybe she doesn't KNOW, but she knows something is wrong. I mean, come on: she's been my best friend since like kindergarten. She can totally tell when something is bothering me. We totally bonded in first grade, the day Orville Lockhead dropped trou in front of us in the line to the music room. I was appalled, having never seen male genitalia before. Lilly, however, was unimpressed. She has a brother, you see, so it was no big surprise to her. She just looked Orville straight in the eye and said, "I've seen bigger."

And you know what? Orville never did it again.

So you can see that Lilly and I share a bond that is stronger than mere friendship.

Which was why she took just one look at my face when she sat down at our lunch table today and said, "What's wrong? Something's wrong. It's not Louie, is it? Did Louie eat another sock?"

As if. This is so much more serious. Not that it isn't totally scary when Louie eats a sock. I mean, we have to rush him to the animal hospital and all, and right away, or he could die. A thousand bucks later, we get an old half-digested sock as a souvenir.

But at least the cat is back to normal.

But this? A thousand bucks won't cure *this*. And nothing will ever be back to normal again.

It is so incredibly embarrassing. I mean, that my mom and Mr. Gianini—you know, DID IT.

Worse, that they DID IT without using anything. I mean, please. Who DOES that anymore?

I told Lilly there wasn't anything wrong, that it was just PMS. It was totally embarrassing to admit this in front of my bodyguard, Lars, who was sitting there eating a gyro that Tina Hakim Baba's bodyguard Wahim—Tina has a bodyguard because her father is a sheik who fears that she will be kidnapped by executives from a rival oil company; I have one because . . . well, just because I'm a princess, I guess—had bought from the vendor in front of Ho's Deli across the street from the school.

The thing is, who announces the vagaries of her menstrual cycle in front of her bodyguard?

But what else was I supposed to say?

I noticed Lars totally didn't finish his gyro, though. I think I completely grossed him out.

Could this day get any worse?

Anyway, even then, Lilly didn't drop it. Sometimes she really does remind me of one of those little pug dogs you always see old ladies walking in the park. I mean, not only is her face kind of small and squashed in (in a nice way), but sometimes when she gets hold of something she simply will not let it go.

Like this thing at lunch, for instance. She was all, "If the only thing bothering you is PMS, then why are you writing in your journal so much? I thought you were mad at your mom for giving that to you. I thought you weren't even going to use it."

Which reminds me that I *was* mad at my mom for giving it to me. She gave me this journal because she says I have a lot of pent-up anger and hostility, and I have to get it out somehow, since I'm not in touch with my inner child and have an inherent inability to verbalize my feelings.

I think my mom must have been talking to Lilly's parents, who are both psychoanalysts, at the time.

But then I found out I was the princess of Genovia, and I started using this journal to record my feelings about that, which, looking back at what I wrote, really were pretty hostile.

But that's nothing compared with how I feel now.

Not that I feel *hostile* toward Mr. Gianini and my mother. I mean, they're adults, and all. They can make their own decisions. But don't they see that this is one decision that is going to affect not just them, but everyone around them? I mean, Grandmère is NOT going to like it when she finds out my mother is having ANOTHER child out of wedlock.

And what about my father? He's already had testicular cancer this year. Finding out that the mother of his only child is giving birth to another man's baby just might kill him. Not that he's still in love with my mom, or anything like that. I don't think.

And what about Fat Louie? How is he going to react to having a baby in the house? He is starved enough for affection as it is, considering I'm the only person who remembers to feed him. He might try to run away, or maybe move up from eating just socks to eating the remote control or something.

I guess I wouldn't mind, though, having a little sister or brother. It might be cool, actually. If it's a girl, I'd share my room with her. I could give her bubble baths and dress her up the way Tina Hakim Baba and I dressed up her little sisters—and her little brother, too, now that I think of it.

I don't think I want a little brother. Tina Hakim Baba told me that baby boys pee in your face when you try to change them. That is so disgusting I don't even want to think about it.

You would think my mother might have considered things like this before deciding to have sex with Mr. Gianini.

And what about that, anyway? How many dates has my mom even been on with Mr. G, anyway? Not many. I mean, like eight, maybe. Eight dates, and it turns out she's already slept with him? And probably a couple of times, because thirty-six-year-old women do not get pregnant just like that. I know, because I can't pick up a copy of *New York* magazine without seeing about a gazillion ads from victims of early menopause who are looking for egg donations from younger women.

But not my mom. Oh, no. Ripe as a mango, that's my mom.

I should have known, of course. I mean, what about that morning I walked out into the kitchen and Mr. Gianini was standing there in his boxer shorts?

I was trying to repress that memory, but I guess it didn't work.

Also, has she even thought about her folic acid intake? I know for a fact she has not. And may I just point out that alfalfa sprouts can be deadly for a newly developing fetus? We have alfalfa sprouts in our refrigerator. Our refrigerator is a deathtrap for a gestating child. There is BEER in the vegetable crisper.

My mother may think she is a fit parent, but she has a lot to learn. When I get home, I fully intend to show her all this information I've printed out off the Web. If she thinks she can put the health of my future baby sister at risk by eating alfalfa sprouts in her sandwiches and drinking coffee and stuff, she is in for a big surprise.

Lilly caught me looking up stuff about pregnancy on the Internet.

She said, "Oh, my God! Is there something about your date with Josh Richter that you didn't tell me?"

Which I really didn't appreciate, since she said it right in front of her brother Michael—not to mention Lars, Boris Pelkowski, and the rest of the class. She said it really loud, too.

You know, these kinds of things wouldn't happen if the teachers at this school would do their jobs and actually teach once in a while. I mean, except for Mr. Gianini, every teacher in this school seems to think it is perfectly acceptable to toss out an assignment and then leave the room to go have a smoke in the teachers' lounge.

Which is probably a health violation, you know.

And Mrs. Hill is the worst of all. I mean, I know Gifted and Talented isn't a real class at all. It's more like study hall for the socially impaired. But if Mrs. Hill would be in here once in a while to supervise, people like me who are neither gifted nor talented and only ended up in this class because they happen to be flunking Algebra and need the extra study time might not get picked on all the time by the resident geniuses.

Because the truth is, Lilly knows perfectly well that the only thing that went on during my date with Josh Richter was that I found out that Josh Richter was totally using me, just because I happen to be a princess and he thought he could get his picture on the cover of *Teen Beat*. I mean, it wasn't like we were ever even alone with each other, unless you count when we were in the car, which I don't, since Lars was there, too, looking out for Euro-trash terrorists who might feel compelled to kidnap me.

Anyway, I exited really fast from the You and Your Pregnancy site I had been looking at, but not fast enough for Lilly. She kept going, "Oh, my God, Mia, why didn't you tell me?"

It was getting kind of embarrassing, even though I explained that I was doing an extra-credit report for Biology, which isn't really a lie, since my lab partner, Kenny Showalter, and I are ethically opposed to dissecting frogs—which the class would be doing next—and Mrs. Sing said we could do a term paper instead.

Only the term paper is supposed to be on the life cycle of the mealworm. But Lilly doesn't know that.

I tried to change the subject by asking Lilly if she knew the truth about alfalfa sprouts, but she just kept blabbing on and on about me and Josh Richter. I really wouldn't have minded so much if it hadn't been for her brother Michael sitting right there, listening instead of working on his webzine, *Crackhead*, like he was supposed to be doing. I mean, it's not like I haven't had a crush on him since forever.

Not that he's noticed, of course. To him, I'm just his kid sister's best friend, that's all. He has to be nice to me, or Lilly will tell everyone in school how she once caught him getting teary-eyed over an old *7th Heaven* rerun.

Besides which, I'm just a lowly freshman. Michael Moscovitz is a senior and has the best grade point average in the whole school (after Lilly) and is covaledictorian of his class. And he didn't inherit the squashed-in-face gene, like his sister. Michael could go out with any girl at Albert Einstein High School that he wanted to.

Well, except for the cheerleaders. They only date jocks.

Not that Michael isn't athletic. I mean, he doesn't believe in organized sports, but he has excellent quadriceps. All his ceps are nice, actually. I noticed last time he came into Lilly's room to yell at us for screaming obscenities too loudly during a Christina Aguilera video, and he didn't happen to be wearing a shirt.

So I really didn't appreciate Lilly standing there talking about how I might be pregnant, right in front of her brother.

TOP FIVE REASONS WHY IT'S HARD BEING BEST FRIENDS WITH A CERTIFIED GENIUS

1. She uses a lot of words I don't understand.
2. She is often incapable of admitting that I might make a meaningful contribution to any conversation or activity.
3. In group situations, she has trouble relinquishing control.
4. Unlike normal people, when solving a problem, she does not go from A to B, but from A to D, making it difficult for us lower human life forms to follow along.
5. You can't tell her anything without her analyzing it half to death.

HOMEWORK

Algebra: problems on pg. 133

English: write a brief family history

World Civ: find an example of negative stereotyping of Arabs (film, television, literature) and submit with explanatory essay

G&T: N/A

French: ecrivez une vignette parisiene

Biology: reproductive system (get answers from Kenny)

ENGLISH JOURNAL

My Family History

The ancestry of my family on my father's side can be traced back to A.D. 568. That is the year when a Visigothic warlord named Albion, who appeared to be suffering from what today would be called an authoritarian personality disorder, killed the king of Italy and all these other people, then made himself king. And after he made himself king, he decided to marry Rosagunde, the daughter of one of the old king's generals.

Only Rosagunde didn't much like Albion after he made her drink wine out of her dead dad's skull, and so she got back at him the night of their wedding by strangling him with her braids while he slept.

With Albion dead, the old king of Italy's son took over. He was so grateful to Rosagunde that he made her princess of an area that is today known as the country of Genovia. According to the only existing records of that time, Rosagunde was a kind and thoughtful ruler. She is my great-grandmother times about sixty. She is one of the primary reasons why today Genovia has some of the best literacy, infant mortality, and employment rates in all of Europe: Rosagunde implemented a highly sophisticated (for its time) system of governmental checks and balances, and did away entirely with the death penalty.

On my mom's side of the family, the Thermopolises were goat herders on the island of Crete until the year 1904, when Dionysius Thermopolis, my mom's great-grandfather, couldn't take it anymore, and ran away to

America. He eventually settled in Versailles, Indiana, where he opened an appliance store. His offspring have been running the Handy Dandy Hardware store on the Versailles, Indiana, courthouse square ever since. My mom says her upbringing would have been much less oppressive, not to mention more liberal, back in Crete.

A Suggested Daily Diet for Pregnancy

• Two to four protein servings of meat, fish, poultry, cheese, tofu, eggs, or nut-grain-bean-dairy combinations
• One quart of milk (whole, skim, buttermilk) or milk equivalents (cheese, yogurt, cottage cheese)
• One or two vitamin C–rich foods: whole potato, grapefruit, orange, melon, green pepper, cabbage, strawberries, fruit, orange juice
• A yellow or orange fruit or vegetable
• Four to five slices of whole-grain bread, pancakes, tortillas, cornbread, or a serving of whole-grain cereal or pasta. Use wheat germ and brewers' yeast to fortify other foods.
• Butter, fortified margarine, vegetable oil
• Six to eight glasses of liquid: fruit and vegetable juices, water, and herb teas. Avoid sugar-sweetened juices and colas, alcohol, and caffeine.
• For snacks: dried fruits, nuts, pumpkin and sunflower seeds, popcorn

My mom is so not going to go for this. Unless she can smother it in hoisin sauce from Number One Noodle Son, she is just not interested.

TO DO BEFORE MOM GETS HOME

Throw out:
Heineken
cooking sherry
alfalfa sprouts
Colombian roast
chocolate chips
salami
Don't forget the
bottle of Absolut
in the freezer!

Buy:
multivitamins
fresh fruit
wheat germ
yogurt

Just when I thought things couldn't get any worse, suddenly, they did.

Grandmère called.

This is so unfair. I thought she was supposed to have gone to Baden-Baden for a little R and R. I was fully looking forward to a respite from her torture sessions—also known as princess lessons, which I am forced by my father, the despot, to attend. I mean, I could use a little vacation myself. Do they really think anyone in Genovia cares whether I know how to use a fish fork? Or if I can sit down without getting wrinkles in the back of my skirt? Or if I know how to say thank you in Swahili? Shouldn't my future countrymen and women be more concerned with my views on the environment? And gun control? And overpopulation?

But according to Grandmère, the people of Genovia don't care about any of that. They just want to know that I won't embarrass them at any state dinners.

As if. Grandmère's the one they should be worried about. I mean, *I* didn't have eyeliner permanently tatooed onto *my* eyelids. *I* don't dress up *my* pet in chinchilla bolero jackets. *I* was never a close personal friend of Richard Nixon.

But oh, no, it's *me* everyone is supposedly so worried about. Like *I* might commit some huge social gaffe at my introduction to the Genovian people in December.

Right.

But whatever. It turns out she didn't go after all, on account of the Baden-Baden baggage handlers being on strike.

I wish I knew the head of the baggage handlers' union in Baden-Baden. If I did, I would totally offer him the one hundred dollars per day my dad has been donating in my name to Greenpeace for performing my duties as princess of Genovia, just so he and the other baggage handlers would go back to work, and get Grandmère out of my hair for a while.

Anyway, Grandmère left a very scary message on the answering machine. She says she has a "surprise" for me. I'm supposed to call her right away.

I wonder what her surprise is. Knowing Grandmère, it's probably something totally horrible, like a coat made out of the skin of baby poodles.

Hey, I wouldn't put it past her.

I'm going to pretend I didn't get the message.

Just got off the phone with Grandmère. She wanted to know why I hadn't returned her call. I told her I didn't get the message.

Why am I such a liar? I mean, I can't even tell the truth about the simplest things. And I'm supposed to be a princess, for crying out loud. What kind of princess goes around lying all the time?

Anyway, Grandmère says she is sending a limo to pick me up. She and my dad and I are going to have dinner in her suite at the Plaza. Grandmère says she is going to tell me all about my surprise then.

Tell me all about it. Not *show me*. Which hopefully rules out the puppy-skin coat.

I guess it's just as well I'm having dinner with Grandmère tonight. My mom invited Mr. Gianini over to the loft tonight so they can "talk." She's not very happy with me for throwing out the coffee and beer (I didn't actually throw it away. I gave it to our neighbor Ronnie). Now my mom is stomping around complaining that she has nothing to offer Mr. G when he comes over.

I pointed out that it's for her own good, and that if Mr. Gianini is any sort of gentleman he'll give up beer and coffee anyway, to support her in her time of need. I know I would expect the father of my unborn child to pay me that courtesy.

That is, in the unlikely event that I were ever actually to have sex.

Some surprise *that* was.

Somebody really needs to tell Grandmère that surprises are supposed to be pleasant. There is nothing pleasant about the fact that she has managed to wrangle a prime-time interview for me with Beverly Bellerieve on *TwentyFour/Seven*.

I don't care if it *is* the most highly rated television news show in America. I told Grandmère a million times I don't want to have my picture taken, let alone be on TV. I mean, it's bad enough that everyone I know is aware that I look like a walking Q-tip, what with my lack of breasts and my Yield-sign–shaped hair. I don't need all of America finding it out.

But now Grandmère says it's my duty as a member of the Genovian royal family. And this time she got my dad into the act. He was all, "Your grandmother's right, Mia."

So I get to spend next Saturday afternoon being interviewed by Beverly Bellerieve.

I told Grandmère I thought this interview thing was a really bad idea. I told her I wasn't ready for anything this big yet. I said maybe we could start small, and have Carson Daly or somebody like that interview me.

But Grandmère didn't go for it. I never met anybody who needed to go to Baden-Baden so badly for a little rest and relaxation. Grandmère looks about as relaxed as Fat Louie right after the vet sticks his thermometer you know where in order to take his temperature.

Of course, this might have had something to do with the fact that Grandmère shaves off her eyebrows and draws on new ones every morning. Don't ask me why. I mean, she has perfectly good eyebrows. I've seen the stubble. But lately I've noticed those eyebrows are getting drawn on higher and higher up her forehead, which gives her this look of perpetual surprise. I think that's because of all her plastic surgeries. If she doesn't watch it, one of these days her eyelids are going to be up in the vicinity of her frontal lobes.

And my dad was no help at all. He was asking all these questions about Beverly Bellerieve, like was it true she was Miss America in 1991 and did Grandmère happen to know if she (Beverly) was still going out with Ted Turner, or was that over?

I swear, for a guy who only has one testicle, my dad sure spends a lot of time thinking about sex.

We argued about it all through dinner. Like were they going to shoot the interview at the hotel, or back in the loft? If they shot it at the hotel, people would be given a false impression about my lifestyle. But if they shot it at the loft, Grandmère insisted, people would be horrified by the squalor in which my mother has brought me up.

Which is totally unfair. The loft is not squalid. It just has that nice, lived-in look.

"Never-been-cleaned look, you mean," Grandmère said, correcting me. But that isn't true, because just the other day I Lemon Pledged the whole place.

"With that animal living there, I don't know how you can ever get the place really clean," Grandmère said.

But Fat Louie isn't responsible for the mess. Dust, as everyone knows, is 95 percent human skin tissue.

The only good thing that I can see about all this is that

at least the film crew isn't going to follow me around at school and stuff. That's one thing to be thankful for, anyway. I mean, could you imagine them filming me being tortured by Lana Weinberger during Algebra? She would so totally start flipping her cheerleading pom-poms in my face, or something, just to show the producers what a wimp I can be sometimes. People all over America would be, like, What is wrong with that girl? Why isn't she self-actualized?

And what about G and T? In addition to there being absolutely no teacher supervision in that class, there's the whole thing with us locking Boris Pelkowski in the supply closet so we don't have to listen to him practice his violin. That has to be some kind of violation of Haz-mat codes.

Anyway, the whole time we were arguing about it, a part of my brain was going, *Right now, as we're sitting here arguing over this whole interview thing, fifty-seven blocks away, my mother is breaking the news to her lover—my Algebra teacher—that she is pregnant with his child.*

What was Mr. G going to say? I wondered. If he expressed anything but joy, I was going to sic Lars on him. I really was. Lars would beat up Mr. G for me, and he probably wouldn't charge me very much for it, either. He has three ex-wives he's paying alimony to, so he can always use an extra ten bucks, which is all I can afford to pay a hired thug.

I really need to see about getting more of an allowance. I mean, who ever heard of a princess who only gets ten bucks a week spending money? You can't even go to the movies on that.

Well, you can, but you can't get popcorn.

The thing is, though, now that I'm back at the loft, I can't tell whether I will need Lars to beat up my Algebra teacher or not. Mr. G and my mom are talking in hushed voices in her room.

I can't hear anything going on in there, even when I press my ear to the door.

I hope Mr. G takes it well. He's the nicest guy my mom's ever dated, despite that F he almost gave me. I don't think he'll do anything stupid, like dump her, or try to sue for full custody.

Then again, he's a man, so who knows?

It's funny, because as I'm writing this, an instant message comes over my computer. It's from Michael! He writes:

CRACKING: What was with you at school today? It was like you were off in this whole other world or something.

I write back:

FTLOUIE: I don't have the slightest idea what you are talking about. Nothing is wrong with me. I'm totally fine.

I am such a liar.

CRACKING: Well, I got the impression that you didn't hear a word that I said about negative slopes.

Since I found out my destiny is to rule a small European principality someday, I have been trying really hard to understand Algebra, as I know I will need it to balance the budget of Genovia, and all. So I have been attending review sessions every day after school, and during Gifted and Talented, Michael has been helping me a little, too.

It's very hard to pay attention when Michael tutors me. This is because he smells really, really good.

How can I think about negative slopes when this guy I've had a major crush on since, oh, I don't know—forever practically, is sitting there right next to me, smelling like soap and sometimes brushing my knee with his?

I reply:

FtLouie: I heard everything you said about negative slopes. Given slope m, +y-intercept (0,b) equation y+mx+b Slope-intercept.
CracKing: WHAT???
FtLouie: Isn't that right?
CracKing: Did you copy that out of the back of the book?

Of course.
Uh-oh, my mom is at the door.

My mom came in. I thought Mr. G had left, so I went, "How'd it go?"

Then I saw she had tears in her eyes, so I went over and gave her this big hug.

"It's okay, Mom," I said. "You'll always have me. I'll help with everything, the midnight feedings, the diaper changing, everything. Even if it turns out to be a boy."

My mom hugged me back, but it turned out she wasn't crying because she was sad. She was crying because she was so happy.

"Oh, Mia," she said. "We want you to be the first to know."

Then she pulled me out into the living room. Mr. Gianini was standing there with this really dopey look on his face. Dopey happy.

I knew before she said it, but I pretended to be surprised anyway.

"We're getting married!"

My mom pulled me into this big group hug between her and Mr. G.

It's sort of weird to be hugged by your Algebra teacher. That's all I have to say.

Tuesday, October 21, 1 a.m.

Hey, I thought my mom was a feminist who didn't believe in the male hierarchy and was against the subjugation and obfuscation of the female identity that marriage necessarily entails.

At least, that's what she always used to say when I asked her why she and my dad didn't ever get married.

I always thought it's because he just never asked her.

Maybe that's why she told me not to tell anyone just yet. She wants to let my dad know in her own way, she says.

All of this excitement has given me a headache.

Oh, my God. I just realized that if my mom marries Mr. Gianini, it means he'll be living here. I mean, my mom would never move to Brooklyn, where he lives. She always says the subway aggravates her antipathy toward the corporate hordes.

I can't believe it. I'm going to have to eat breakfast every morning with my *Algebra teacher*.

And what happens if I accidentally see him naked, or something? My mind could be permanently scarred.

I'd better make sure the lock on the bathroom door is fixed before he moves in.

Now my throat hurts, in addition to my head.

When I woke up this morning, my throat hurt so much, I couldn't even talk. I could only croak.

I tried croaking for my mom for a while, but she couldn't hear me. So then I tried banging on the wall, but all that did was make my Greenpeace poster fall down.

Finally I had no choice but to get up. I wrapped my comforter around me so I wouldn't get a chill and get even sicker, and went down the hall to my mom's room.

To my horror, there was not one lump in my mom's bed, but TWO!!!! Mr. Gianini stayed over!!!!

Oh, well. It's not like he hasn't already promised to make an honest woman of her.

Still, it's a little embarrassing to stumble into your mom's bedroom at six in the morning and find your *Algebra teacher* in there with her. I mean, that kind of thing might warp a lesser person than myself.

But whatever. I stood there croaking in the doorway, totally too freaked out to go in, and finally my mom cracked an eye open. Then I whispered to her that I was sick, and told her that she'd have to call the attendance office and explain that I wouldn't be in school today.

I also asked her to call and cancel my limo, and to let Lilly know we wouldn't be stopping by to pick her up.

I also told her that if she was going to go to the studio, she'd have to get my dad or Lars (please not Grandmère) to come to the loft and make sure no one tried to kidnap or assassinate me while she was gone and I was in my weakened physical state.

I think she understood me, but it was hard to tell.

I tell you, this princess business is no joke.

My mom stayed home from the studio today.

I croaked to her that she shouldn't. She has a show at the Mary Boone Gallery in about a month, and I know she only has about half the paintings done that she's supposed to have. If she should happen to succumb to morning sickness, she is one dead realist.

But she stayed home anyway. I think she feels guilty. I think she thinks my getting sick is her fault. Like all my anxiety over the state of her womb weakened my autoimmune system, or something.

Which totally isn't true. I'm sure whatever it is I have, I picked it up at school. Albert Einstein High School is one giant petri dish of bacteria, if you ask me, what with the astonishing number of mouth-breathers who go there.

Anyway, about every ten minutes, my guilt-ridden mother comes in and asks me if I want anything. I forgot she has a Florence Nightingale complex. She keeps making me tea, and cinnamon toast with the crusts cut off. This is very nice, I must say.

Except then she tried to get me to let some zinc dissolve on my tongue, as one of her friends told her this is supposedly a good way to combat the common cold.

That was not so nice.

She felt bad about it when the zinc made me gag a whole bunch. She even ran down to the deli and bought me one of those king-size Crunch bars to make up for it.

Later she tried to make me bacon and eggs in order to build up my strength, but there I drew the line: Just because

I'm on my deathbed does not mean it's okay to abandon all of my vegetarian principles.

My mother just took my temperature. Ninety-nine point six.

If this were medieval times, I would probably be dead.

TEMPERATURE CHART
11:45 a.m.—99.2
12:14 p.m.—99.1
1:27 p.m.—98.6

This stupid thermometer must be broken!

2:05 p.m.—99.0
3:35 p.m.—99.1

Clearly, if this keeps up, I will be unable to be interviewed by Beverly Bellerieve on Saturday.

YIPPEE!!!

Even later on Tuesday

Lilly just stopped by. She brought me all of my home-work. She says I look wretched, and that I sound like Linda Blair in *The Exorcist*. I've never seen *The Exorcist*, so I don't know if this is true or not. I don't like movies where people's heads spin around, or where things come bursting out of their stomachs. I like movies with beauty makeovers and dancing.

Anyway, Lilly says that the big news at school is that the "It Couple," Josh Richter and Lana Weinberger, got back together, after having been broken up one whole entire week (a personal record for the both of them: Last time they broke up, it was for only three days). Lilly says when she went by my locker to get my books, Lana was standing there in her cheerleader uniform, waiting for Josh, whose locker is next to mine.

Then, when Josh showed up, he laid a big wet one on Lana that Lilly swears was the equivalent to an F5 on the Fujimoto scale of tornado suck zone intensity, making it impossible for Lilly to close my locker door again (how well I know that problem). Lilly resolved the situation pretty quickly, however, by accidentally-on-purpose stabbing Josh in the spine with the tip of her number two pencil.

I thought about telling Lilly my own Big News: you know, about my mom and Mr. G. I mean, she's going to find out about it anyway.

Maybe it was the infection coursing through my body, but I just couldn't bring myself to do it. I just couldn't bear the thought of what Lilly might say regarding the potential size of my future brother's or sister's nostrils.

Anyway, I have about a ton of homework. Even the father of my unborn sibling, who you would think would feel an iota of sympathy toward me, loaded me down with it. I tell you, there isn't a single perk to having your mother engaged to your Algebra teacher. Not a single one.

Well, except when he comes over for dinner and helps me with the assignment. He doesn't give me the answers, though, so I mostly get sixty-eights. And that's still a D.

And I am really sick now! My temperature has gone up to ninety-nine point eight! Soon it will reach one hundred.

If this were an episode of *ER*, they'd have practically put me on a respirator already.

There is no way I'll be able to be interviewed by Beverly Bellerieve now. NO WAY.

Tee hee.

My mom has her humidifier in here, going on full blast. Lilly says my room is just like Vietnam, and why don't I at least crack the window, for God's sake.

I never thought of it before, but Lilly and Grandmère sort of have a lot in common. For instance, Grandmère called a little while ago. When I told her how sick I was, and how I probably wouldn't be able to make it to the interview on Saturday, she actually *chastised* me.

That's right. Chastised me, like it was *my* fault I got sick. Then she starts going on about how on her wedding day she had a fever of one hundred and two, but did she let that stop her from standing through a two-hour wedding ceremony, then riding in an open coach through the streets of Genovia waving to the populace, and then dining on prosciutto and melon at her reception and waltzing until four in the morning?

No, you might not be too surprised to learn. It did not.

That, Grandmère said, is because a princess does not use poor health as an excuse to shirk her duties to her people.

As if the people of Genovia care about my doing some lousy interview for *Twenty-Four/Seven*. They don't even get that show there. I mean, except for the people who have satellite dishes, maybe.

Lilly is just about as unsympathetic as Grandmère. In fact, Lilly isn't really a very soothing visitor to have at all when you are sick. She suggested that it was possible that I have consumption, just like Elizabeth Barrett Browning. I said I thought it was probably only bronchitis, and Lilly said that's probably what Elizabeth Barrett Browning thought, too, before she died.

HOMEWORK

Algebra: problems at the end of Chapter 10
English: in your journal, list your favorite TV show, movie, book, food, etc.
World Civ: one thousand word essay explaining the conflict between Iran and Afghanistan
G&T: as if
French: ecrivez une vignette amusant (Oh, right)
Biology: endocrine system (get answers from Kenny)

God! What are they trying to do over there, anyway? Kill me?

Wednesday, October 22

This morning my mom called my dad where he's staying at the Plaza, and made him bring the limo over so I could go to the doctor. This is because when she took my temperature after I woke up, it was one hundred and two, just like Grandmère's on her wedding day.

Only I can tell you, I didn't feel much like waltzing. I could hardly even get dressed. I was so feverish I actually put on one of the outfits Grandmère bought me. So there I was in Chanel from head to toe, with my eyes all glassy and this sheen of sweat all over me. My dad jumped about a foot and a half when he saw me, I think because he thought for a minute that I *was* Grandmère.

Only of course I am much taller than Grandmère. Though my hair isn't as big.

It turns out that Dr. Fung is one of the few people in America who hadn't heard yet that I'm a princess, so we had to sit in the waiting room for like ten minutes before he could see me. My dad spent the ten minutes talking to the receptionist. That's because she was wearing an outfit that showed her navel, even though it is practically winter.

And even though my dad is completely bald and wears suits all the time instead of khakis like a normal dad, you could tell the receptionist was completely into him. That's because in spite of his incipient European-ness, my dad is still something of a hottie.

Lars, who is also a hottie in a different sort of way (being extremely large and hairy), sat next to me, reading *Parenting* magazine. I could tell he would have preferred the latest copy of *Soldier of Fortune*, but they don't have a subscription to that at the SoHo Family Medical Practice.

Finally Dr. Fung saw me. He took my temperature (101.7) and felt my glands to see if they were swollen (they were). Then he tried to take a throat culture to check for strep.

Only when he jabbed that thing into my throat, it made me gag so hard, I started coughing uncontrollably. I couldn't stop coughing, so I told him between coughs that I was going to get a drink of water. I think I must have been delusional because of my fever and all, since what I did instead of getting water was walk right out of the doctor's office. I got back into the limo and told the chauffeur to take me to Emerald Planet right away, so I could get a smoothie.

Fortunately the chauffeur knew better than to take me somewhere without my bodyguard. He got on the radio and said some stuff, and then Lars came out to the limo with my dad, who asked me what on earth I thought I was doing.

I thought about asking him the exact same thing, only about the receptionist with the pierced belly button. But my throat hurt too much to talk.

Dr. Fung was pretty nice about it in the end. He gave up on the throat culture and just prescribed some antibiotics and this cough syrup with codeine in it—but not until he had one of his nurses take a picture of us shaking hands together inside the limo so he could hang it on his wall of celebrity photos. He has pictures of himself up there shaking hands with other famous patients of his, like Robert Goulet and Lou Reed.

Now that my raging fever has gone down, I can see that

I was behaving completely irrationally. I would have to say that that trip to the doctor's office was probably one of the most embarrassing moments of my life. Of course, there've been so many, it's hard to tell where this one ranks. I think I would chalk it up there with the time I accidentally dropped my dinner plate in the buffet line at Lilly's bat mitzvah, and everybody kept stepping in gefiltefish for the rest of the night.

MIA THERMOPOLIS'S TOP FIVE MOST EMBARRASSING MOMENTS

1. Josh Richter kissing me in front of the whole school while everyone looked at me.
2. The time when I was six and Grandmère ordered me to hug her sister, Tante Jean Marie, and I started to cry because I was afraid of Jean Marie's mustache, and hurt Jean Marie's feelings.
3. The time when I was seven and Grandmère forced me to attend a boring cocktail party she gave for all her friends, and I was so bored I picked up this little ivory coaster holder which was shaped like a rickshaw, and then I wheeled it around the coffee table, making noises like I was speaking Chinese, until all the coasters fell out the back of the rickshaw and rolled around on the floor very noisily, and everyone looked at me. (This is even more embarrassing when I think of it now, because imitating Chinese people is very rude, not to mention politically incorrect.)
4. The time when I was ten and Grandmère took me

and some of my cousins to the beach and I forgot my bikini top and Grandmère wouldn't let me go back to the chateau to get it, she said this was France for God's sake and I should just go topless like everybody else, and even though I didn't have anything more up there to show than I do now, I was mortified and wouldn't take my shirt off and everyone looked at me because they thought I had a rash or disfiguring birthmark or a shriveled-up Siamese-twin fetus hanging off me.

5. The time when I was twelve and I got my first period, and I was at Grandmère's house and I had to tell her about it because I didn't have any pads or anything, and later that night as I walked in for dinner I overheard Grandmère telling all her friends about it, and then for the rest of the night all they did was make jokes about the wonder of womanhood.

Now that I think about it, almost all of the most embarrassing moments of my life have something to do with Grandmère.

I wonder what Lilly's parents, who are both psychoanalysts, would have to say about this.

TEMPERATURE CHART

5:20 p.m.—99.3
6:45 p.m.—99.2
7:52 p.m.—99.1

Is it possible I am getting better *already*? This is horrible. If I get better, I'll have to go on that stupid interview. . . .

This calls for drastic measures: Tonight I fully intend to take a shower and stick my head out the window with my hair wet.

That will show them.

Oh, my God. Something so exciting just happened, I can hardly write.

This morning as I was lying in my sickbed, my mom handed me a letter that she said had come in the mail yesterday, only she forgot to give it to me.

This wasn't like the electricity or cable bills my mom usually forgets about after they have arrived. This was a personal letter to me.

Still, since the address on the front of it was typed, I didn't suspect anything out of the ordinary. I thought it was a letter from school, or something. Like maybe I'd made honor roll (HA HA). Except that there was no return address, and usually mail from Albert Einstein High School has Albert's thoughtful face in the left-hand corner, along with the school's address.

So you can imagine my surprise when I opened the letter and found not a flier asking me to show my school spirit by making rice krispy treats to help raise money for the crew team but the following . . . which, for want of a better word, I can only call a love letter:

> *Dear Mia* (the letter went)
> *I know you will think it's strange, receiving a letter like this. I feel strange writing it. And yet I am too shy to tell you face-to-face what I'm about to tell you now: And that's that I think you are the Josiest girl I've ever met.*
> *I just want to make sure you know that there's one*

person, anyway, who liked you long before he found out
you were a princess . . .

And will keep on liking you, no matter what.

Sincerely,
A Friend

Oh, my God!

I couldn't believe it! I'd never gotten a letter like this before. Who could it be from? I seriously couldn't figure it out. The letter was typed, like the address on the envelope. Not by a typewriter, either, but obviously on a computer.

So even if I wanted to compare keystrokes, say, on a suspect's typewriter (like Jan did on *The Brady Bunch* when she suspected Alice of sending her that locket), I couldn't. You can't compare the type on laser printers, for God's sake. It's always the same.

But who could have sent me such a thing?

Of course, I know who I *want* to have sent it.

But the chances of a guy like Michael Moscovitz ever actually liking me as more than just a friend are like zero. I mean, if he liked me, he had a perfect opportunity to say something about it the night of the Cultural Diversity dance, when he was so nice to step in and ask me to dance, after Josh Richter dogged me so hard. And we didn't just dance once, either. We danced a few times. Slow dances, too. And after the dance, we hung out in his room at the Moscovitzes' apartment. He could have said something then, if he'd wanted to.

But he didn't. He didn't say a thing about liking me.

And why would he? I mean, I am a complete freak, what with my noticeable lack of mammary glands, my gigantism, and my utter inability ever to mold my hair into something remotely resembling a style.

We just got through studying people like me in Bio, as a matter of fact. Biological sports, we are called. A biological sport occurs when an organism shows a marked change from the normal type or parent stock, typically as a result of mutation.

That is me. That is so totally me. I mean, if you looked at me, and then you looked at my parents, who are both very attractive people, you would be all, What *happened*?

Seriously. I should go live with the X-men, I am such a mutant.

Besides, is Michael Moscovitz really the type of guy who'd say I was the *Josiest* girl in school? I mean, I am assuming the author is referring to Josie, the lead singer of Josie and the Pussycats, played by Rachael Leigh Cook in the movie. Except that in no way do I resemble Rachael Leigh Cook. I wish. *Josie and the Pussycats* started out as a cartoon about a girl band that solves crimes, like on *Scooby Doo*, and Michael doesn't even watch the Cartoon Network, as far as I know.

Michael generally only watches PBS, the Sci Fi Channel, and *Buffy the Vampire Slayer*. Maybe if the letter had said *I think you are the* Buffiest *girl I've ever met*. . . .

But if it isn't from Michael, who could it be from?

This is all so exciting, I want to call someone and tell them. Only who? Everyone I know is in school.

WHY DID I HAVE TO GET SICK????

Forget sticking my wet head out the window. I have to get better right away so I can go back to school and figure out who my secret admirer is!

TEMPERATURE CHART:
10:45 a.m.—99.2
11:15 a.m.—99.1
12:27 p.m.—98.6

Yes! YES! I am getting better! Thank you, Selman Waksman, inventor of the antibiotic.

2:05 p.m.—99.0

No. Oh, no.

3:35 p.m.—99.1

Why is this happening to me?

Later on Thursday

This afternoon while I was lying around with icepacks under the covers, trying to bring my fever down so I can go to school tomorrow and find out who my secret admirer is, I happened to see the best episode of *Baywatch* ever.

Really.

See, Mitch met this girl with this very fake French accent during a boat race, and they totally fell in love and ran around in the waves to this excellent soundtrack, and then it turned out the girl was engaged to Mitch's opponent in the boat race—and not only that—she was actually the *princess of this small European country Mitch had never heard of*. Her fiancé was this prince her father had betrothed her to at birth!

While I was watching this, Lilly came over with my new homework assignments, and she started watching with me, and she totally missed the deep philosophical importance of the episode. All she said was, "Boy, does that royal chick need an eyebrow waxing."

I was appalled.

"Lilly," I croaked. "Can't you see that this episode of *Baywatch* is prophetic? It is entirely possible that I have been betrothed since birth to some prince I've never even met, and my dad just hasn't told me yet. And I could very likely meet some lifeguard on a beach and fall madly in love with him, but it won't matter, because I will have to do my duty and marry the man my people have picked out for me."

Lilly said, "Hello, exactly how much of that cough medicine have you had today? It says one *tea*spoon every four hours, not *table*spoon, dorkus."

I was annoyed at Lilly for failing to see the bigger picture. I couldn't, of course, tell her about the letter I'd gotten. Because what if her brother was the one who wrote it? I wouldn't want him thinking I'd gone blabbing about it to everyone I knew. A love letter is a very private thing.

But still, you would think she'd be able to see it from my perspective.

"Don't you understand?" I rasped. "What is the point of me liking anybody, when it's entirely possible that my dad has arranged a marriage for me with some prince I've never met? Some guy who lives in, like, Dubai, or somewhere, and who gazes daily at my picture and longs for the day when he can finally make me his own?"

Lilly said she thought I'd been reading too many of my friend Tina Hakim Baba's teen romances. I will admit, that is sort of where I got the idea. But that is not the point.

"Seriously, Lilly," I said. "I have to guard diligently against falling in love with somebody like David Hasselhoff or your brother, because in the end I might have to marry Prince William." Not that that would be such a great sacrifice, and all.

Lilly got up off my bed and stomped out into the loft's living room. My dad was the only one around, because when he'd come over to check on me, my mom had suddenly remembered an errand she had to get done and dashed off.

Only of course there was no errand. My mom still hasn't told my dad about Mr. G and her pregnancy, and how they're getting married, and all. I think she's afraid that he might start yelling at her for being so irresponsible (which I could totally see him doing).

So instead she flees from Dad in guilt every time she sees him. It would almost be funny, if it wasn't such a pathetic way for a thirty-six-year-old woman to behave. When I am thirty-six, I fully intend to be self-actualized, so you will not catch me doing any of the things my mother is always doing.

"Mr. Renaldo," I heard Lilly say, as she went out into the living room. She calls my dad Mr. Renaldo even though she knows perfectly well he is the prince of Genovia. She doesn't care though, because she says this is America and she isn't calling anybody "Your Highness." She is fundamentally opposed to monarchies—and principalities, like Genovia, fall under that heading. Lilly believes that sovereignty rests with the people. In colonial times, she'd probably have been branded a Whig.

"Mr. Renaldo," I heard her ask my dad. "Is Mia secretly betrothed to some prince somewhere?"

My dad lowered his newspaper. I could hear it crinkling all the way from my bedroom. "Good God, no," he said.

"Moron," she said to me, when she came stomping back into my room. "And while I can see why you might want to guard diligently against falling in love with David Hasselhoff, who is, by the way, old enough to be your father, and hardly a hottie, what does my *brother* have to do with any of this?"

Too late, I realized what I'd said. Lilly has no idea how I feel about her brother Michael. Actually, *I* don't really have any idea about how I feel about him either. Except that he looks extremely Casper Van Dien with his shirt off.

I *so* want him to be the one who'd written that letter. I really, really do.

But I'm not about to mention this to his sister.

Instead, I told her I think it unfair of her to demand explanations for stuff I said under the influence of codeine cough syrup.

Lilly just got that expression she gets sometimes when teachers ask a question and she knows the answer, only she wants to give someone else in the class a chance to answer for a change.

It really can be exhausting sometimes, having a best friend with an IQ of 170.

HOMEWORK

Algebra: problems 1–20, pg. 115
English: Chapter 4 of Strunk and White
World Civ: two-hundred–word essay on the conflict between India and Pakistan
G&T: Yeah, right
French: Chaptre huit
Biology: pituitary gland (ask Kenny!)

LILLY MOSCOVITZ AND MIA THERMOPOLIS'S
LIST OF CELEBRITIES AND THEIR BREASTS

CELEBRITY	LILLY	MIA
Britney Spears	Fake	Real
Jennifer Love Hewitt	Fake	Real
Winona Ryder	Fake	Real
Courtney Love	Fake	Fake
Jennie Garth	Fake	Real
Tori Spelling	Fake	Fake
Brandy	Fake	Real
Neve Campbell	Fake	Real
Sarah Michelle Gellar	Real	Real
Christina Aguilera	Fake	Real
Lucy Lawless	Real	Real
Melissa Joan Hart	Fake	Real
Mariah Carey	Fake	Fake
Rachael Leigh Cook	Fake	Real

Even later on Thursday

After dinner I felt well enough to get out of bed, and so I did.

I checked my e-mail. I was hoping there might be something from my mysterious "friend." If he knew my "snail mail" address, I figured he'd know my e-mail address, too. Both are listed in the school directory.

Tina Hakim Baba was one of the people who e-mailed me. She sent get-well wishes. So did Shameeka. Shameeka mentioned that she was trying to talk her father into letting her have a Halloween party, and that if she succeeded, would I come? I wrote back to say of course, if I wasn't too weak from coughing.

There was also a message from Michael. It was a get-well message, too, but it was animated, like a little film. It showed a cat that looked a lot like Fat Louie doing a little get-well dance. It was very cute. Michael signed it "Love, Michael."

Not Sincerely.

Not Yours Truly.

Love.

I played it four times, but I still couldn't tell whether he was the one who'd sent me that letter. The letter, I noticed, never once mentioned the word *love.* It said the sender *liked* me. And he signed it "sincerely."

But there was no love. Not a hint of love.

Then I saw a message from someone whose e-mail address I didn't recognize. Oh, my God! Could it be my anonymous liker? My fingers were trembling on my mouse. . . .

And then I opened it and saw the following message from JoCrox:

JoCRox: Just a note to say hope you are feeling better. Missed you in school today! Did you get my letter? Hope it made you feel at least a little better, knowing there's someone out there who thinks you rock. Get well soon.
Your Friend

Oh, my God! It's *him*! My anonymous admirer!

But who is Jo Crox? I don't know anyone named Jo Crox. He says he missed me in school today, which means we might be in a class together. But there are no Jo's in any of my classes.

Maybe Jo Crox isn't really his name. In fact, Jo Crox doesn't sound like a name at all. Maybe that actually stands for Joc Rox.

But I don't know any jocks, either. I mean, not personally.

Oh, no, wait, I get it:

Jo-C-rox.

Josie Rocks! Oh, my God! Josie from *Josie and the Pussycats*!

That is just so *cute*.

But who? *Who is it*?

I figured there was only one way to find out, so I wrote back right away:

FtLOUIE: Dear Friend, I got your letter. Thank you very much. Thanks also for the get-well wishes.

WHO ARE YOU? (I swear I won't tell anyone.)
Mia

I sat around for half an hour, hoping he would write back, but he never did.

WHO IS IT??? WHO IS IT??

I have GOT to get well by tomorrow so I can go to school and figure out who Jo-C-rox is. Otherwise, I will go mental, just like Mel Gibson's girlfriend in *Hamlet*, and I'll end up floating in my Lanz of Salzburg nightie in the Hudson with the rest of the medical waste.

Friday, October 24, Algebra

I AM BETTER!!!!!

Well, actually, I don't feel all that great, but I don't care. I don't have a temperature, so my mother had no choice but to let me go to school. There was no way I was going to lie in bed another day. Not with Jo-C-rox out there somewhere, possibly loving me.

But so far, nothing. I mean, we swung by Lilly's in the limo and picked her up, as usual, and Michael was with her and all, but by the casual way he said hello to me you would hardly have known that he'd ever sent me a get-well e-mail signed "Love, Michael," let alone ever called me the Josiest girl he's ever met. It is so very clear that he isn't Jo-C-rox.

And that *Love* at the end of his e-mail was just a platonic *Love*. I mean, Michael's *Love* obviously didn't mean he actually *loves* me.

Not that I ever thought he did. Or might. Love me, I mean.

He did walk me to my locker, though. This was extremely nice of him. Granted, we were in the middle of a heated discussion about Tuesday's episode of *Buffy the Vampire Slayer*, but still, no boy has ever walked me to my locker before. Boris Pelkowski meets Lilly at the front doors to the school and walks her to her locker *every single morning*, and has done so ever since the day she agreed to be his girlfriend.

Okay, I admit that Boris Pelkowski is a mouth-breather who continues to tuck his sweaters into his pants despite my frequent hints that in America, this is considered a *Glamour*

"Don't." But still, he is a boy. And it is always cool to have a boy—even one who wears a retainer—walk you to your locker. I know I have Lars, but it's different having your *bodyguard* walk you to your locker, as opposed to an actual *boy*.

I just noticed that Lana Weinberger has purchased all new notebook binders. I guess she threw away the old ones. She had written "Mrs. Josh Richter" all over them, then crossed it out when she and Josh broke up. They are back together now. I guess she's willing once again to have her identity obfuscated by taking her "husband's" name, since she's already got three *I Love Josh*es and seven *Mrs. Josh Richter*s on her Algebra notebook alone.

Before class started, Lana was telling everyone who would listen about some party she is going to tonight. None of us are invited, of course. It's a party given by one of Josh's friends.

I never get invited to parties like that. You know, like the ones in movies about teenagers, where somebody's parents go out of town, so everybody in the school comes over with kegs of beer and trashes the house?

I do not actually know anybody who lives in a house. Just apartment buildings. And if you start trashing an apartment, you can bet the people next door will call the doorman to complain. That could get you in major trouble with the co-op board.

I don't suppose Lana has ever considered these things, however.

The 3rd power of x is called cube of x
The 2nd power of x is squared

Ode to the View from the
Window in My Algebra Class

Sun-warmed concrete benches
next to tables with built-in checkerboards
and the graffiti left by hundreds
before us in
Day-Glo spray paint:

Joanne Loves Richie
Punx Rule
Nuke Fags and Lesbos
And
Amber Is a Slut.

The dead leaves and plastic bags scatter
in the breeze from the park
and men in business suits try to keep the
last few remaining strands of hair covering
their pink bald spots.
Cigarette packets and used-up chewing gum
coat the gray sidewalk.

And I think
What does it matter
that it is not a linear equation if any variable is raised to
a power?
We're all just going to die anyway.

LIST FIVE BASIC TYPES OF GOVERNMENT

anarchy
monarchy
aristocracy
dictatorship
oligarchy
democracy

LIST FIVE PEOPLE WHO COULD
CONCEIVABLY BE JO-C-ROX

Michael Moscovitz (I wish)
Boris Pelkowski (please no)
Mr. Gianini (in a misguided attempt to cheer me up)
My dad (ditto)
That weird boy I see sometimes in the cafeteria who
gets so upset whenever they serve chili and there's corn
in it (please please no)

AAAAARRRRRGGGGGGHHHHHH!!!!!!!!!!!!!

Friday, October 24, G & T

It turns out that since I've been gone, Boris has started learning some new music on his violin. Right now he is playing a concerto by someone named Bartok.

And let me tell you, that's exactly how it sounds. Even though we locked him and his violin into the supply closet, it isn't doing any good. You can't even hear yourself think. Michael had to go to the nurse's office for ibuprofen.

But before he left, I tried to steer the conversation in the direction of mail. You know, casually, and all.

Just in case.

Anyway, Lilly was talking about her show, *Lilly Tells It Like It Is*, and I asked her if she's still getting a lot of fan mail—one of her biggest fans, her stalker Norman, sends her free stuff all the time, with the understanding that he wants her to show her bare feet on the air: Norman is a foot fetishist.

Then I mentioned that I'd received some *intriguing* mail lately. . . .

Then I looked at Michael real fast, to see how he responded.

But he didn't even glance up from his laptop.

And now he is back from the nurse's office. She wouldn't give him any ibuprofen because it is a violation of the school drug code. So I gave him some of my codeine cough syrup. He says it cleared his headache right up.

But that might also have been because Boris knocked over a can of paint thinner with his bow and we had to let him out of the supply closet.

HERE IS WHAT I HAVE TO DO

1. Stop thinking so much about Jo-C-rox
2. Ditto Michael Moscovitz
3. Ditto my mother and her reproductive issues
4. Ditto my interview tomorrow with Beverly Bellerieve
5. Ditto Grandmère
6. Have more self-confidence
7. Stop biting off fake fingernails
8. Self-actualize
9. Pay more attention in Algebra
10. Wash PE shorts

Later on Friday

Talk about embarrassing! Principal Gupta somehow found out about my giving Michael some of my codeine cough syrup, and I got called out of Bio and sent to her office to discuss my trafficking of controlled substances on school grounds!

Oh, my God! I really and truly thought I was going to get expelled then and there.

I explained to her about the ibuprofen and the Bartok, but Principal Gupta was totally unsympathetic. Even when I brought up all the kids who stand outside the school and smoke. Do they get in trouble for bumming cigarettes off one another?

And what about the cheerleaders and their Dexatrim?

But Principal Gupta said cigarettes and Dexatrim are different from narcotics. She took my codeine cough syrup away and told me I could have it back after school. She also told me not to bring it to school on Monday.

She doesn't have to worry. I was so embarrassed about the whole thing, I am seriously considering never coming back to school at all, let alone on Monday.

I don't see why I can't be home-schooled, like the boys from Hanson. Look how they turned out.

HOMEWORK

Algebra: problems on pg. 129
English: describe an experience that moved you profoundly

World Civ: two hundred words on the rise of the
Taliban in Afghanistan
G&T: *Please*
French: devoirs—les notes grammaticals: 141–143
Biology: central nervous system

ENGLISH JOURNAL

My Favorite Things

FOOD

Vegetarian lasagna

MOVIE

My favorite movie of all time is one I first saw on HBO when I was twelve. It has remained my favorite movie in spite of my friends' and family's efforts to introduce me to so-called finer examples of cinematic art. Quite frankly, I think that *Dirty Dancing*, starring Patrick Swayze and a pre–nose-job Jennifer Grey, has everything films like *Breathless* and *September*, created by supposed "auteurs" of the medium, lack. For instance, *Dirty Dancing* takes place at a summer resort. Movies that take place in resorts (other good examples include *Cocktail* and *Aspen Extreme*) are just plain better, I've noticed, than other movies. Also, *Dirty Dancing* has dancing. Dancing in movies is always good. Think how much better Oscar Award–winning films, like *The English Patient*, would be if they had dancing in them. I am always so much less bored at the movies when there are people dancing on the screen. So all I have to say to the many, many people who disagree with me about *Dirty Dancing* is: "Nobody puts Baby in the corner."

TV SHOW

My favorite TV show is *Baywatch*. I know people think it is very lame and sexist, but actually it isn't. The boys are as scantily clad as the girls, and in the later episodes at least, a woman is in charge of the whole life-guarding operation. And the truth of the matter is, whenever I watch this show, I feel happy. That is because I know whatever jam Hobie gets into, whether it is giant electric eels or emerald smugglers, Mitch will get him out of it, and everything will be done to an excellent soundtrack, and with stunning shots of the ocean. I wish there was a Mitch in my life to make everything all right at the end of the day.

Also that my breasts were as big as Carmen Electra's.

BOOK

My favorite book is called *IQ 83*. It is by the best-selling author of *The Swarm*, Arthur Herzog. *IQ 83* is about a bunch of doctors who mess around with DNA, and they unwittingly cause an accident that makes everyone in the world lose a bunch of IQ points and start acting dumb. Seriously! Even the president of the United States. He ends up drooling like an idiot! And it's up to Dr. James Healey to save the country from being populated by a bunch of overweight morons who do nothing but watch Jerry Springer and eat Ho Hos all day. This book has never gotten the attention it should receive. It hasn't even been made into a movie!

This is a literary travesty.

Even later on Friday

What am I supposed to do about this stupid English journal assignment, *Describe an experience that moved you profoundly?* I am so sure. What do I write about? The time I walked into the kitchen and found my Algebra teacher standing there in his underwear? That didn't move me, exactly, but it was certainly an experience.

Or should I talk about the time my dad spilled his guts about how it turns out I am the heir to the throne of the principality of Genovia? That was an experience, although I don't know if it was profound, and even though I was crying, I don't think it was because I was moved. I was just mad nobody had told me before. I mean, I guess I can understand that it might be embarrassing for him to have to admit to the Genovian people that he had a child out of wedlock, but to hide that fact for fourteen years? Talk about denial.

My Bio partner Kenny, who also has Mrs. Spears for English, says he is going to write about his family's trip to India last summer. He contracted cholera there, and nearly died. As he lay in his hospital bed in that far-off foreign land, he realized that we are only on this planet for a short while, and that it is vital we use every moment we have left as if it were our last. That is why Kenny is devoting his life to finding a cure for cancer, and promoting Japanese anime.

Kenny is so lucky. If only I could contract a potentially fatal disease.

I am beginning to realize that the only thing profound about my life so far is its complete and utter lack of profundity.

Jefferson Market
The freshest produce—guaranteed
Fast, Free Delivery

Order no. 2764

1 package soybean curd
1 bottle wheat germ
1 loaf whole-grain bread
5 grapefruits
12 oranges
1 bunch bananas
1 package brewer's yeast
1 quart skim milk
1 quart orange juice (not from concentrate)
1 pound butter
1 dozen eggs
1 bag unsalted sunflower seeds
1 box whole-grain cereal
Toilet paper
Q-tips

Deliver to:
Mia Thermopolis, 1005 Thompson Street, #4A

Saturday, October 25, 2 p.m., Grandmère's suite

I am sitting here waiting for my interview. In addition to my throat hurting, I feel like I am going to throw up. Maybe my bronchitis has turned into the flu, or something. Maybe the falafel I ordered in for dinner last night was made from rotten chickpeas, or something.

Or maybe I'm just totally nervous, since this interview is going to be broadcast to an estimated 22 million homes on Monday night.

Although I find it very hard to believe that 22 million families could possibly be interested in anything *I* have to say.

I read that when Prince William gets interviewed, he gets the questions about a week before, so he has time to think up really smart and incisive answers. Apparently, members of the Genovian royal family are not extended that same courtesy. Not that even with a week's worth of notice I could ever think of anything smart and incisive. Well, okay, maybe smart, but definitely not incisive.

Well, probably not even smart, either, depending on what they ask.

So I am sitting here and I really do feel like I am going to throw up, and I wish I could hurry up and get this over with. It was supposed to start two hours ago.

But Grandmère isn't satisfied with the way the cosmetic technician (makeup lady) did my eyes. She says I look like a *poulet*. That means "hooker" in French. Or chicken. But when my Grandmère says it, it always means hooker.

Why can't I have a nice, normal grandma, who makes

rugelach and thinks I look wonderful no matter what I have on? Lilly's grandma has never said the word *hooker* in her life, even in Yiddish. I know that for a fact.

So the makeup lady had to go down to the hotel gift shop to see if they have any blue eyeshadow. Grandmère wants blue, because she says it matches my eyes. Except that my eyes are gray. I wonder if Grandmère is color-blind.

That would explain a lot.

I met Beverly Bellerieve. The one good thing about all this is that she actually seems semi-human. She told me that if she asked anything that I felt was too personal or embarrassing, that I could just say I don't want to answer. Isn't that nice?

Plus she is very beautiful. You should see my dad. I can already tell that Beverly is going to be this week's girlfriend. Well, she's better than the women he usually hangs around with. At least Beverly looks as if she probably isn't wearing a thong. And as if her brainstem is fully functional.

So, considering that Beverly Bellerieve turns out to be so nice and all, you'd think I wouldn't be so nervous.

And truthfully, I'm not so sure it's just the interview that's making me feel like I'm going to hurl. It's actually something my dad said to me, when I came in. It was the first time I'd seen him since the time he spent at the loft while I was sick. Anyway, he asked me how I was feeling and all, and I lied and said fine, and then he said, "Mia, is your Algebra teacher—"

And I was all, "Is my Algebra teacher what?" thinking he was going to ask me if Mr. Gianini was teaching me about parallel numbers.

But that is so totally NOT what he asked me. Instead, he asked me, "Is your Algebra teacher living in the loft?"

Well, I was so shocked, I didn't know what to say. Because of course Mr. Gianini isn't living there. Not really.

But he will be. And probably pretty shortly, too.

So I just went, "Um, no."

And my dad looked relieved! He actually looked relieved!

So how is he going to look when he finds out the *truth*?

It is very hard to concentrate on the fact that I am about to be interviewed by this world-renowned television news journalist, when all I can think about is how my poor dad is going to feel when he finds out my mother is marrying my Algebra teacher and also having his baby. Not that I think my dad still loves my mom, or anything. It's just that, as Lilly once pointed out, his chronic bed-hopping is a clear indication that he has some serious intimacy issues.

And with Grandmère as a mother, you can see why that might be.

I think he really would like to have what my mom has with Mr. Gianini. Who knows how he is going to take the news about their impending marriage, when my mom finally works up the guts to tell him? He might completely freak out. He might even want me to come live with him in Genovia, to comfort him in his grief!

And of course I will have to say yes, because he is my dad and I love him, and all.

Except that I really don't want to live in Genovia. I mean, I would miss Lilly and Tina Hakim Baba and all my other friends. And what about Jo-C-rox? How would I ever find out who he is? And what about Fat Louie? Would I get to keep him, or what? He is very well behaved (except when it comes to ingesting socks, and that whole thing with the sparkly objects) and if there was a rodent problem in the castle, he would totally solve it. But what if they don't let cats in the palace? I mean, he hasn't had his claws removed, so if there's any sort of valuable furniture or tapestries or whatever, you can pretty much kiss them good-bye. . . .

Mr. G and my mom are already talking about where his stuff is going to go when he moves into the loft. And Mr. G has some really cool-sounding stuff. Like a foozball table, a drum set (who knew Mr. Gianini was *musical*?), a pinball machine, AND a 36-inch flat-screen TV.

I am not even kidding. He is *way* cooler than I ever thought.

If I move to Genovia, I will totally miss out on having my own foozball table.

But if I don't move to Genovia, who will comfort my poor dad in his chronic loneliness?

Oops, the cosmetic technician is back with the blue eye-shadow.

I swear I am going to heave. Good thing I was too nervous to eat anything all day.

Oh, God, oh, God, oh, God, oh, God, oh, God, OH, GOD.

I screwed up. I REALLY screwed up.

I don't know what happened. I honestly don't. Everything was going along fine. I mean, that Beverly Bellerieve, she's so . . . *nice.* I was really, really nervous, and she did her very best to try to calm me down.

Still, I think I did some major babbling.

Think??? I KNOW I did.

I didn't mean for it to happen. I really didn't. I don't even know how it slipped out. I was just so nervous and hyper, and there were those lights and that microphone and everything. I felt like . . . I don't know. Like I was back in Principal Gupta's office, living through that whole codeine cough-syrup thing again.

So when Beverly Bellerieve said, "Mia, didn't you have some exciting news recently?" I totally freaked out. Part of me was like, How did she know? And another part of me was like, Millions of people are going to see this. Act happy.

So I went, "Oh. Yes. Well, I'm pretty excited. I've always wanted to be a big sister. But they don't really want to make a big deal out of it, you know. It's just going to be a very small ceremony at City Hall, with me as their witness—"

That's when my dad dropped the glass of Perrier he'd been drinking. Then Grandmère started hyperventilating and had to breathe into a paper bag.

And I sat there going, Oh, my God. Oh, my God, what have I done?

Of course it turned out that Beverly Bellerieve hadn't been referring to my mother's pregnancy at all. Of course not. How could she have known about it?

What she'd actually been referring to, of course, was my F in Algebra being raised to a D.

I tried to get up and go to my dad to comfort him, since I could see he'd sunk into a chair and had his head in his hands. But I was all tangled up in my microphone wires. It had taken about half an hour for the sound guys to get the wires right, and I didn't want to mess them up or anything, but I could see that my dad's shoulders were shaking, and I was sure he was crying, just like he always does at the end of *Free Willy*, though he tries to pretend it's just allergies.

Beverly, seeing this, made a slashing motion with her hand to the camera guys, and very nicely helped me get untangled.

But when I finally got to my dad, I saw he wasn't crying. . . . But he certainly didn't look too good. He didn't sound very good, either, when he croaked for someone to bring him a whiskey.

After three or four gulps, though, he got a little of his color back. Which is more than I can say for Grandmère. I don't think she will ever recover. Last time I saw her, she was downing a Sidecar that someone had dropped some Alka-Seltzer tablets into.

I don't even want to think about what my mom is going to say when she finds out what I've done. I mean, even though my dad said not to worry, that he'll explain to Mom what happened, I don't know. He had kind of a weird look on his face. I hope he doesn't plan on popping Mr. G one in the piehole.

Me and my big mouth. My HUGE, GROTESQUE, DISPROPORTIONATELY MASSIVE mouth.

There's no telling what else I said, once the interview got underway again. I was so completely freaked out by that first thing, I can't remember a single other thing Beverly Bellerieve might have asked me.

My dad has assured me that he's not the least bit jealous of Mr. Gianini, that he is very happy for my mother, and that he thinks she and Mr. G make a great couple. I think he means it. He seemed pretty unfazed, after the initial shock. Once the interview was over, I noticed that he and Beverly Bellerieve were yukking it up quite a bit.

All I can say is, thank goodness I am going straight from the hotel to Lilly's. She is having us all over to film next week's episode of her show. I think I'll see if I can spend the night. Maybe this way, by the time my mom sees me tomorrow, she'll have had time to process the whole thing, and will have forgiven me.

I hope.

Sunday, October 26, 2 a.m., Lilly's bedroom

Okay, I just have one question: Why does it always have to go from bad to worse for me?

I mean, apparently it is not enough that

1. I was born lacking any sort of mammary growth gland
2. My feet are as long as a normal person's thigh
3. I'm the sole heir to the throne of a European principality
4. My grade point average is still slipping in spite of everything
5. I have a secret admirer who will not declare himself
6. My mother is pregnant with my Algebra teacher's baby, and
7. All of America is going to know it after Monday night's broadcast of my exclusive interview on *Twenty-Four/Seven*

No, in addition to all of that, I happen to be the only one of my friends who still has yet to be French-kissed.

Seriously. For next week's show, Lilly insisted on shooting what she calls a Scorsesian confessional, in which she hopes to illustrate the degenerate lows to which today's youth have sunk. So she made us all confess to the camera our worst sins, and it turns out Shameeka, Tina Hakim Baba, Ling Su, and Lilly have ALL had boys' tongues in their mouths. *All of them.*

Except for me.

Okay, I'm not so surprised about Shameeka. Ever since she grew breasts over the summer, boys have been buzzing around her like she was the newest version of Tomb Raider, or something. And Ling Su and that Clifford guy she has been seeing are way into each other.

But Tina? I mean, she has a bodyguard, just like me. When has *she* ever been alone long enough with a boy for him to French her?

And Lilly? Excuse me, but Lilly, MY BEST FRIEND? Who I thought tells me everything (even though I don't necessarily always return the favor)? She has known the touch of a boy's tongue upon her own, and she never thought to tell me until NOW?

Boris Pelkowski is apparently a much smoother operator than you would suspect, considering that whole sweater thing.

I am sorry, but that is just sick. Sick, sick, sick, sick. I would rather die a dried-up, never-been-kissed old maid than be French-kissed by Boris Pelkowski. I mean, he always has FOOD in his retainer. And not just any food, either, but usually weird, multicolored foods like Gummi Bears and Jelly Bellies.

Lilly says he takes his retainer out when they kiss, though.

God, I am such a reject. The only boy who has ever kissed me did it just so he could get his picture in the paper.

Yeah, there was some tongue action, but believe me, I kept my lips way closed.

And since I have never been French-kissed, and had nothing good to confess on the show, Lilly decided to punish me by giving me a Dare. She didn't even ask me if I would prefer a Truth.

Lilly dared me I wouldn't drop an eggplant onto the sidewalk from her sixteenth-story bedroom window.

I said I most certainly would, even though of course, I totally didn't want to. I mean, how stupid. Somebody could seriously get hurt. I am all for illustrating the degenerate lows to which America's teens have sunk, but I wouldn't want anybody to get their head bashed in.

But what could I do? It was a Dare. I had to go along with it. I mean, it's bad enough I've never been Frenched. I don't want to be branded a wimp, too.

And I couldn't exactly stand there and go, well, all right, I may never have been French-kissed by a boy, but I have been the recipient of a love letter that was written by one. A boy, I mean.

Because what if Michael is Jo-C-rox? I mean, I know he probably isn't, but . . . well, what if he is? I don't want Lilly to know—any more than I want her to know about my interview with Beverly Bellerieve, or the fact that my mom and Mr. G are getting married. I am trying very hard to be a normal girl, and frankly, none of the aforementioned can be even remotely construed as normal.

I guess the knowledge that somewhere in the world there is a boy who likes me gave me a sense of empowerment—something I certainly could have used during my interview with Beverly Bellerieve, but whatever. I may not be able to form a coherent sentence when there is a television camera aimed in my direction, but I am at least capable, I decided, of throwing an eggplant out the window.

Lilly was shocked. I had never accepted a Dare like that before.

I can't really explain why I did it. Maybe I was just trying to live up to my new reputation as a very Josie-ish type of girl.

Or maybe I was more scared of what Lilly would try to make me do if I said no. Once she made me run up and down the hallway naked. Not the hallway in the Moscovitzes' apartment, either. The hallway *outside* of it.

Whatever my reasons, I soon found myself sneaking past the Drs. Moscovitz—who were lounging around in sweatpants in the living room, with stacks of important medical journals all around their chairs—though Lilly's father was reading a copy of *Sports Illustrated* and Lilly's mom was reading *Cosmo*—and creeping into the kitchen.

"Hello, Mia," Lilly's father called from behind his magazine. "How are you doing?"

"Um," I said, nervously. "Fine."

"And how is your mother?" Lilly's mother asked.

"She's fine," I said.

"Is she still seeing your Algebra teacher in a social capacity?"

"Um, yes, Dr. Moscovitz," I said. More than you know.

"And are you still amenable to the relationship?" Lilly's father wanted to know.

"Um," I said. "Yes, Dr. Moscovitz." I didn't think it would be appropriate to mention the whole thing about how my mom is having Mr. G's baby. I mean, I was supposed to be on a Dare, after all. You aren't supposed to stop for psychoanalysis when you are on a Dare.

"Well, tell her hello from me," Lilly's mother said. "We can't wait until her next show. It's at the Mary Boone Gallery, right?"

"Yes, ma'am," I said. The Moscovitzes are big fans of my mother's work. One of her best paintings, *Woman Enjoying a Quick Snack at Starbucks*, is hanging in their dining room.

"We'll be there," Lilly's father said.

Then he and his wife turned back to their magazines, so I hurried into the kitchen.

I found an eggplant in the vegetable crisper. I hid it under my shirt so the Drs. Moscovitz wouldn't see me sneaking back into their daughter's room holding a giant ovoid fruit, something sure to cause unwanted questions. While I carried it, I thought, *This is how my mother is going to look in a few months*. It wasn't a very comforting thought. I don't think my mother is going to dress any more conservatively while pregnant than she did not pregnant.

Which is to say, not very.

Then, while Lilly narrated gravely into the microphone about how Mia Thermopolis was about to strike a blow for good girls everywhere, and Shameeka filmed, I opened the window, made sure no innocent bystanders were below, and then. . . .

"Bomb's away," I said, like in the movies.

It *was* kind of cool seeing this huge purple eggplant—it was the size of a football—tumbling over and over in the air as it fell. There are enough streetlamps on Fifth Avenue, where the Moscovitzes live, for us to see it as it plummeted downward, even though it was night. Down and down the eggplant went, past the windows of all the psychoanalysts and investment bankers (the only people who can afford apartments in Lilly's building) until suddenly—

SPLAT!

The eggplant hit the sidewalk.

Only it didn't just hit the sidewalk. It *exploded* on the sidewalk, sending bits of eggplant flying everywhere—mostly all over an M1 city bus that was driving by at the time, but quite a lot all over a Jaguar that had been idling nearby.

While I was leaning out the window, admiring the splatter pattern the eggplant's pulp had made all over the street and sidewalk, the driver-side door of the Jaguar opened up, and a man got out from behind the wheel, just as the doorman to Lilly's building stepped out from beneath the awning over the front doors, and looked up—

Suddenly, someone threw an arm around my waist and yanked me backward, right off my feet.

"Get down!" Michael hissed, pulling me down to the parquet.

We all ducked. Well, Lilly, Michael, Shameeka, Ling Su, and Tina ducked. I was already on the floor.

Where had Michael come from? I hadn't even known he was home—and I'd asked, believe me, on account of the whole running-down-the-hallway-naked thing. Just in case, and all.

But Lilly had said he was at a lecture on quasars over at Columbia and wouldn't be home for hours.

"Are you guys stupid, or what?" Michael wanted to know. "Don't you know, besides the fact that it's a good way to kill someone, it's also against the law to drop things out a window in New York City?"

"Oh, Michael," Lilly said, disgustedly. "Grow up. It was just a common garden vegetable."

"I'm serious." Michael looked mad. "If anyone saw Mia do that just now, she could be arrested."

"No, she couldn't," Lilly said. "She's a minor."

"She could still go to juvenile court. You'd better not be planning on airing that footage on your show," Michael said.

Oh, my God, Michael was defending my honor! Or at least trying to make sure I didn't end up in juvenile court. It was just so sweet. So . . . well, Jo-C-rox of him.

Lilly went, "I most certainly am."

"Well, you'd better edit out the parts that show Mia's face."

Lilly stuck her chin out. "No way."

"Lilly, everybody knows who Mia is. If you air that segment, it will be all over the news that the princess of Genovia was caught on tape dropping projectiles out the window of her friend's high-rise apartment. Get a clue, will you?"

Michael had let go of my waist, I noticed, with regret.

"Lilly, Michael's right," Tina Hakim Baba said. "We better edit that part out. Mia doesn't need any more publicity than she has already."

And Tina didn't even *know* about the *TwentyFour/Seven* thing.

Lilly got up and stomped back toward the window. She started to lean out—checking, I guess, to see whether the doorman and the owner of the Jaguar were still there— but Michael jerked her back.

"Rule Number One," he said. "If you insist on dropping something out the window, never, ever check to see if anybody is standing down there, looking up. They will see you look out and figure out what apartment you are in. Then you will be blamed for dropping whatever it was. Because no one but the guilty party would be looking out the window under such circumstances."

"Wow, Michael," Shameeka said admiringly. "You sound like you've done this before."

Not only that. He sounded like Dirty Harry.

Which was just how I felt when I dropped that eggplant out the window. Like Dirty Harry.

And it had felt good—but not quite so good as having Michael rush to my defense like that.

Michael said, "Let's just say I used to have a very keen interest in experimenting with the earth's gravitational pull."

Wow. There is so much I don't know about Lilly's brother. Like he used to be a juvenile delinquent!

Could a computer genius-slash-juvenile delinquent ever be interested in a flat-chested princess like myself? He did save my life tonight (well, okay: he saved me from possible community service).

It's not a French kiss, or a slow dance, or even an admission he's the author of that anonymous letter.

But it's a start.

I know what yer thinkin':
Did he fire six shots, or only five?
Frankly, in all the confusion,
I kinda lost track myself.
But you gotta ask yourself one question:

(*beat*)

Do I feel lucky?

(*long pause*)

Well?

(*long pause*)

Do ya, punk?

THINGS TO DO

1. English journal
2. Stop thinking about that stupid letter
3. Ditto Michael Moscovitz
4. Ditto the interview
5. Ditto Mom
6. Change cat litter
7. Drop off laundry
8. Get super to put lock on bathroom door
9. Buy: Dishwashing liquid
     Q-tips
     Canvas stretchers (for Mom)
     That stuff you put on your fingernails that
     makes them taste bad
     Something nice for Mr. Gianini, to say
     welcome to the family
     Something nice for Dad, to say don't worry,
     someday you, too, will find true love

Sunday, October 26, 7 p.m.

I was really afraid that when I got home my mom was going to be disappointed in me.

Not *yell* at me. My mom is really not a yelling kind of person.

But she does get disappointed in me, like when I do something stupid like not call and tell her where I am if I am out late (which, given my social life, or lack thereof, hardly ever happens).

But I did screw up this time, and big time. It was really, really hard to leave the Moscovitzes' apartment this morning and come home, knowing the potential for disappointment that awaited me there.

Of course, it's always hard to leave Lilly's. Every time I go there, it's like taking a vacation from my real life. Lilly has such a nice, normal family. Well, as normal as two psychoanalysts whose son has his own webzine and whose daughter has her own cable-access television show can be. At the Moscovitzes', the biggest problem is always whose turn is it to walk Pavlov, their sheltie, or whether to order Chinese or Thai take-out.

At my house, the problems always seem to be a little more complicated.

But of course when I finally did work up the courage to come home, my mom was totally happy to see me. She gave me a big hug, and told me not to worry about what had happened at the interview taping. She said Dad had talked to her, and that she completely understood. She even tried to get me to believe that it was *her* fault for not having said anything to him right away.

Which I know isn't true—it's still my fault, me and my idiot mouth—but it was nice to hear, just the same.

So then we had a nice, fun time sitting around planning her and Mr. G's wedding. My mom decided Halloween would be an excellent day to get married, because the idea of marriage is so scary. Since it was going to be at City Hall, that meant I'd probably have to skip school, but that was okay by me!

Since it would be Halloween, my mom decided that instead of a wedding dress, she would go to the courthouse dressed as King Kong. She wants me to dress up as the Empire State Building (God knows I am tall enough). She was trying to convince Mr. G to dress as Fay Ray when the phone rang, and she said it was Lilly, for me.

I was surprised, since I had just left Lilly's, but I figured I must have left my toothbrush there, or something.

But that wasn't why she was calling. That wasn't why she was calling at all—as I found out when she demanded tartly, "What's this I hear about you being interviewed on *TwentyFour/Seven* this week?"

I was stunned. I actually thought Lilly had ESP or something, and had been hiding it from me all these years. I said, "How did you know?"

"Because there are commercials announcing it every five minutes, dorkus."

I switched on the TV. Lilly was right! No matter what station you put it on, there were ads urging viewers to "tune in tomorrow night" to see Beverly Bellerieve's exclusive interview with "America's royal, Princess Mia."

Oh, my God. My life is so over.

"So why didn't you tell me you are going to be on TV?" Lilly wanted to know.

"I don't know," I said, feeling like I was going to throw up all over again. "It just happened yesterday. It's no big deal."

Lilly started yelling so loud I had to hold the phone away from my ear.

"NO BIG DEAL??? You were interviewed by Beverly Bellerieve and it was NO BIG DEAL??? Don't you realize that BEVERLY BELLERIEVE IS ONE OF AMERICA'S MOST POPULAR AND HARDEST-HITTING JOURNALISTS, and that she is my all-time ROLE MODEL and HERO???"

When she finally calmed down enough to let me talk, I tried to explain to Lilly that I had no idea about Beverly's journalistic merits, much less that she was Lilly's all-time role model and hero. She just seemed, I said, like a very nice lady.

By that time, Lilly was totally fed up with me. She said, "The only reason I'm not mad at you is that tomorrow you are going to tell me every single little detail about it."

"I am?"

Then I asked a more important question. "Why should you be mad at me?" I really wanted to know.

"Because you gave me exclusive first rights to interview you," Lilly pointed out. "For *Lilly Tells It Like It Is*."

I have no memory of this, but I guess it must be true.

Grandmère, I could see from the ads, had been right about the blue eyeshadow. Which was surprising, because she's never been right about much else.

TOP FIVE THINGS GRANDMÈRE HAS BEEN WRONG ABOUT

1. That my dad would settle down when he met the right woman.
2. That Fat Louie would suck out my breath and suffocate me as I slept.
3. That if I didn't attend an all-girls school, I would contract a social disease.
4. That if I got my ears pierced, they would get infected and I would die of blood poisoning.
5. That my figure would fill out by the time I hit my teens.

Sunday, October 26, 8 p.m.

You will not believe what got delivered to our house while I was gone. I was sure it was a mistake, until I saw the following attached. I am going to kill my mother.

Jefferson Market
The freshest produce—guaranteed
Fast, Free Delivery

Order no. 2803

1 package microwave cheese popcorn
1 case Yoo Hoo chocolate drink
1 jar cocktail olives
1 bag Oreos
1 container fudge ripple ice cream
1 package all-beef hot dogs
1 package hot-dog buns
1 package string cheese
1 bag milk chocolate chips
1 bag barbecue potato chips
1 container beer nuts
1 bag Milano cookies
1 jar sweet gherkins
Toilet paper
6-pound ham

Deliver to:
Helen Thermopolis, 1005 Thompson Street, #4A

Hasn't she the slightest idea how adversely all this saturated fat and sodium will affect her unborn child? I can see that Mr. Gianini and I will have to be hypervigilant for the next seven months. I have given everything except the toilet paper to Ronnie, next door. Ronnie says she is going to hand out the junkiest stuff to any trick-or-treaters who might come by. She has to watch her figure since her sex-change operation. Now that she's taking all those estrogen injections, everything goes right to her hips.

Sunday, October 26, 9 p.m.

Another e-mail from Jo-C-rox!
This one went:

JoCrox: Hi, Mia. I just saw the ad for your interview. You look great.
Sorry I can't tell you who I am. I'm surprised you haven't guessed by now. Now stop checking your e-mail and get to work on your Algebra homework. I know how you are about that. It's one of the things I like best about you.
Your Friend

Okay, this is going to drive me insane. Who could it be? Who????

I wrote back right away:

FtLouie: WHO ARE YOU??

I was hoping that would get the point across, but he so totally did not write back. I was trying to figure out who I know who knows that I always wait until the last minute to do my Algebra homework. Unfortunately, though, I think everyone knows it.

But the person who knows it best of all is Michael. I mean, doesn't he help me every day with my Algebra homework in G and T? And he is always chastising me for not putting my carry-overs in straight enough lines and all of that.

If ONLY Jo-C-rox were Michael Moscovitz. If only, if only, if ONLY.

But I'm sure it isn't. That would simply be too good to be true. And really excellent things like that only happen to girls like Lana Weinberger, never to girls like me. Knowing my luck, it will totally be that weird chili guy. Or some guy who breathes through his mouth, like Boris.

WHY ME?

Unfortunately, it appears that Lilly is not the only one who noticed the ads for tonight's broadcast.

Everybody is talking about it. I mean, EVERYBODY.

And everybody says they are going to watch it.

Which means by tomorrow, everyone will know about my mom and Mr. Gianini.

Not that I care. There is nothing to be ashamed of. Nothing at all. Pregnancy is a beautiful and natural thing.

Still, I wish I could remember more about what Beverly and I talked about. Because I am sure my mom's impending marriage is not all we discussed. And I am totally worried I said other stuff that will come off sounding stupid.

I have decided that I should look more closely into that home-schooling idea, just in case. . . .

Tina Hakim Baba told me that her mother, who was a supermodel in England before she married Mr. Hakim Baba, used to get interviewed all the time. Mrs. Hakim Baba says that as a courtesy the interviewers would send her a copy of the tape before it aired, so if she had any objections, she could straighten them out before the thing was broadcast.

This sounded like a good idea, so at lunch I called my dad in his hotel suite and asked him if he could get Beverly to do that for me.

He said, "Hold on," and asked her. It turns out Beverly was right there! In my dad's hotel room! On a Monday afternoon!

Then, to my utter mortification, Beverly Bellerieve actually got on the phone and said, "What's the matter, Mia?"

I told her I was still pretty nervous about the interview, and was there any chance I could see a copy of it before it aired?

Beverly said a bunch of stuff about how adorable I was and how that wouldn't be necessary. Now that I think about it, I can't remember exactly what she said, but I just got this overwhelming feeling that everything would be just fine.

Beverly is just one of those people who make you feel good about yourself. I don't know how she does it.

No wonder my dad hasn't let her out of his hotel room since Saturday.

Two cars, one going north at 40 mph and one going south at 50 mph, leave town at the same time. In how many hours will they be 360 miles apart?

Why does it matter? I mean, really.

Monday, October 27, Bio

Mrs. Sing, our Biology teacher, says it is physiologically impossible to die of either boredom or embarrassment, but I know that isn't true, because I am experiencing heart failure right now.

That is because after G and T, Michael and Lilly and I were walking down the hall together, since Lilly was going to Psych and I was going to Bio and Michael was going to Calc, which are all right across the hall from one another, and Lana Weinberger walked right up to us—RIGHT UP TO MICHAEL AND ME—and held up two of her fingers and waggled them at us, and went, "Are you two going out?"

I could seriously die right now. I mean, you should have seen Michael's face. It was like his head was about to explode, he turned that red.

And I'm sure I wasn't all that pale myself.

Lilly didn't help by letting out this giant horse laugh and going, "As if!"

Which caused Lana and her cronies to burst out laughing, too.

I don't see what's so funny about it. Those girls obviously haven't seen Michael Moscovitz with his shirt off. Believe me, I have.

I guess because the whole thing was so ridiculous and everything, Michael just kind of ignored it. But I'm telling you, it's getting harder and harder for me not to ask him if he is Jo-C-rox. Like I keep trying to find ways to work *Josie and the Pussycats* into the conversation. I know I shouldn't, but I just can't help it!

I don't know how much longer I can stand being the only girl in the ninth grade who doesn't have a boyfriend.

HOMEWORK

Algebra: problems on pg. 135
English: "Make the most of yourself, for that is all there is of you." —Ralph Waldo Emerson
Write feelings about this quote in journal
World Civ: questions at the end of Chapter 9
G&T: N/A
French: plan an itinerary for a make-believe trip to Paris
Biology: Kenny's doing it

Remind Mom to make appointment with licensed geneticist. Could she or Mr. G be a carrier for the genetic mutation Tay-Sachs? It is common in Jews of Eastern European origin and in French Canadians. Are there any French Canadians in our family? FIND OUT!

I never thought I would say this, but I am worried about Grandmère.

I am serious. I think she has officially lost it.

I walked into her hotel suite for my princess lesson today—since I am scheduled to have my official introduction to the Genovian people sometime in December, and Grandmère wants to be sure I don't insult any dignitaries or whatever during it—and guess what Grandmère was doing?

Consulting with the royal Genovian event planner about my mother's wedding.

I am totally serious. Grandmère had the guy flown in. All the way from Genovia! There they sat at the dining table with this huge sheet of paper stretched in front of them, on which were drawn all these circles, and to which Grandmère was attaching these tiny slips of paper. She looked up when I came in and said, in French, "Oh, Amelia. Very nice. Come and sit down. We have much to discuss, you and Vigo and I."

I think my eyes must have been bulging out of my head. I couldn't believe what I was seeing. I was totally hoping what I was seeing was, you know . . . not what I was seeing.

"Grandmère," I said. "What are you *doing*?"

"Isn't it obvious?" Grandmère looked at me with her drawn-on eyebrows raised higher than ever. "Planning a wedding, of course."

I swallowed. This was bad. WAY bad.

"Um," I said. "Whose wedding, Grandmère?"

She looked at me very sarcastically. "Guess," she said.

I swallowed some more. "Uh, Grandmère?" I said. "Can I talk to you a minute? In private?"

But Grandmère just waved her hand and said, "Anything you have to say to me, you can say in front of Vigo. He has been dying to meet you. Vigo, Her Royal Highness, the Princess Amelia Mignonette Grimaldi Renaldo."

She left out the Thermopolis. She always does.

Vigo jumped up from the table and came rushing over to me. He was way shorter than me, about my mom's age, and had on a gray suit. He seemed to share my grandmother's penchant for purple, since he was wearing a lavender shirt in some kind of very shiny material, along with an equally shiny dark purple tie.

"Your Highness," he gushed. "The pleasure is all mine. So delightful finally to meet you." To Grandmère, he said, "You're right, madame, she has the Renaldo nose."

"I told you, did I not?" Grandmère sounded smug. "Uncanny."

"Positively." Vigo made a little picture frame out of his index fingers and thumbs and squinted at me through it.

"Pink," he said, decidedly. "Absolutely pink. I do so love a pink maid of honor. But the other attendants will be in ivory, I think. *So* Diana. But then, Diana was always so *right*."

"It's really nice to meet you," I said to Vigo. "But the thing is, I think my mom and Mr. Gianini were kind of planning on having a private ceremony down at—"

"City Hall." Grandmère rolled her eyes. It is very scary when she does this, because a long time ago, she had black eyeliner tattooed all around her eyelids so she wouldn't have to waste valuable time putting on makeup when she could be, you know, terrorizing someone. "Yes, I heard all about it. It is ridiculous, of course. They will be married in the White and Gold Room at the Plaza, with a reception directly afterward in the Grand Ballroom, as befits the mother of the future regent of Genovia."

"Um," I said. "I really don't think that's what they want."

Grandmère looked incredulous. "Whyever not? Your father is paying for it, of course. And I have been very generous. They are each allowed to invite twenty-five guests."

I looked down at the sheet of paper in front of her. There were way more than fifty slips of paper in front of her.

Grandmère must have noticed the direction of my gaze, since she went, "Well, I, of course, require at least three hundred."

I stared at her. "Three hundred what?"

"Guests, of course."

I could see that I was way out of my depth. I was going to have to call in for reinforcements if I hoped to get anywhere with her.

"Maybe," I said, "I should just give Dad a call and run this by him. . . . "

"Good luck," Grandmère said with a snort. "He went off with that Bellerieve woman, and I haven't heard from him since. If he is not careful, he is going to end up in the same situation as your Algebra teacher over there."

Except it's totally unlikely Dad would be getting anybody pregnant, since the whole reason I was his heir, instead of some legitimately produced offspring, is that he is no longer fertile, due to the massive doses of chemotherapy that cured his testicular cancer. But I suppose Grandmère is still in denial about this, considering what a disappointing heir I've turned out to be.

It was at this point that a strange moaning noise came out from under Grandmère's chair. We both looked down. Rommel, Grandmère's miniature poodle, was cowering in fright at the sight of me.

I know I am hideous and all of that, but really, it's ridiculous how scared that dog is of me. And I love animals!

But even St. Francis of Assisi would have a hard time appreciating Rommel. I mean, first of all, he recently has developed a nervous disorder (if you ask me, it's from living in such close proximity to my grandmother) that made all his fur fall out, so Grandmère dresses him up in little sweaters and coats so he won't catch cold.

Today Rommel had on a mink bolero jacket. I am not even joking. It was dyed lavender to match the one slung across Grandmère's shoulders. It is horrifying enough to see a person wearing fur, but it is a thousand times worse to see an animal wearing another animal's fur.

"Rommel," Grandmère yelled at the dog. "Stop that growling."

Except that Rommel wasn't growling. He was moaning. Moaning with fright. At the sight of me. ME!

How many times in one day must I be humiliated?

"Oh, you stupid dog." Grandmère reached down and picked Rommel up, much to his unhappiness. You could tell her diamond brooches were poking him in the spine (there is no fat on him at all, and since he doesn't have any fur, he is especially sensitive to pointy objects), but even though he wriggled to be free, she wouldn't let go of him.

"Now, Amelia," Grandmère said. "I need your mother and whatever-his-name-is to write their guests' names and addresses down tonight so I can have the invitations messengered tomorrow. I know your mother is going to want to invite some of those more, ahem, free-spirited friends of hers, Mia, but I think it would be better if perhaps if they just stood outside with the reporters and tourists and waved as she climbed in and out of the limo. That way they'll still have a feeling of belonging, but they won't make anyone uncomfortable with their unattractive hairstyles and ill-fitting attire."

"Grandmère," I said. "I really think—"

"And what do you think about this dress?" Grandmère held up a picture of a Vera Wang wedding gown with a big poofy skirt that my mom wouldn't be caught dead in.

Vigo went, "No, no, Your Highness. I really think this is more the thing." Then he held up a photo of a slinky Armani number that my mom similarly wouldn't be caught dead in.

"Uh, Grandmère," I said. "This is all really nice of you, but my mom definitely doesn't want a big wedding. Really. Definitely."

"*Pfuit*," Grandmère said. *Pfuit* is French for "No," duh. "She will when she sees the luscious hors d'œuvres they'll be serving at the reception. Tell her about them, Vigo."

Vigo said with relish: "Truffle-filled mushroom caps, asparagus tips wrapped in salmon slivers, pea pods stuffed with goat cheese, endive with crumbles of blue cheese inside each gently furled leaf. . . ."

I said, "Uh, Grandmère? No, she won't. Believe me."

Grandmère went, "Nonsense. Trust me, Mia, your mother is going to appreciate this someday. Vigo and I will make her wedding day an event she will never forget."

I had no doubt about that.

I said, "Grandmère, Mom and Mr. G were really planning on something very casual and simple—"

But then Grandmère threw me one of those looks of hers—they are really very scary—and said, in this deadly serious voice, "For three years, while your grandfather was off having the time of his life fighting the Germans, I held those Nazis—not to mention Mussolini—at bay. They lobbed mortars at the palace doors. They tried to drive tanks across my moat. And yet I persevered, through sheer willpower alone. Are you telling me, Amelia, that I cannot convince one pregnant woman to see things my way?"

Well, I'm not saying my mom has anything in common with Mussolini or Nazis, but as far as putting up a resistance to Grandmère? I'd place my money on my mom over a fascist foreign dictator any day.

I could see that reasoning wasn't going to be effective in this particular case. So I went along with it, listening to Vigo gush over the menu he had picked out, the music he had selected for the ceremony and later, for the reception—even admiring the portfolio of the photographer he had chosen.

It wasn't until they actually showed me one of the invitations that I realized something.

"The wedding's this Friday?" I squeaked.

"Yes," Grandmère said.

"That's Halloween!" The same day as my mom's court-house wedding. Also, incidentally, the same night as Shameeka's party.

Grandmère looked bored. "What of it?"

"Well, it's just . . . you know. Halloween."

Vigo looked at my grandmother. "What is this Halloween?" he asked. Then I remembered they don't go in for Halloween much in Genovia.

"A pagan holiday," Grandmère replied, with a shudder. "Children dress up in costumes and demand candy from strangers. Horrible American tradition."

"It's in a *week*," I pointed out.

Grandmère raised her drawn-on eyebrows. "And so?"

"Well, that's so . . . you know. Soon. People—" like me "—might have other plans already."

"Not to be indelicate, Your Highness," Vigo said. "But we do want to get the ceremony out of the way before your mother begins to . . . well, *show*."

Great. So even the royal Genovian event organizer knows my mother is expecting. Why doesn't Grandmère just rent the Goodyear blimp and broadcast it all over the tristate area?

Then Grandmère started telling me that, since we were on the topic of weddings and all, it might be a good opportunity for me to start learning what will be expected out of any future consorts I might have.

Wait a minute. "Future *what*?"

"Consorts," Vigo said, excitedly. "The spouse of the reigning monarch. Prince Philip is Queen Elizabeth's *consort.* Whomever you choose to marry, Your Highness, will be *your* consort."

I blinked at him. "I thought you were the royal Genovian event organizer," I said.

"Vigo not only serves as our event organizer, but also the royal protocol expert," Grandmère explained.

"Protocol? I thought that was something to do with the army. . . ."

Grandmère rolled her eyes. "Protocol is the form of ceremony and etiquette observed by foreign dignitaries at state functions. In your case, Vigo can explain the expectations of your future consort. Just so there won't be any unpleasant surprises later."

Then Grandmère made me get out a piece of paper and write down exactly what Vigo said, so that, she informed me, in four years, when I am in college, and I take it into my head to enter into a romantic liaison with someone completely inappropriate, I will know why she is so mad.

College? Grandmère obviously does not know that I am being actively pursued by would-be consorts at this very moment.

Of course, I don't even know Jo-C-rox's real name, but hey, it's something, at least.

Then I found out what, exactly, consorts have to do. And now I sort of doubt I'll be French-kissing anyone soon. In fact, I can totally see why my mother didn't want to marry my dad—that is, if he ever asked her.

I have glued the piece of paper here:

Expectations of any
Royal Consort of the Princess of Genovia

The consort will ask the princess's permission before he leaves the room.

The consort will wait for the princess to finish speaking before speaking himself.

The consort will wait for the princess to lift her fork before lifting his own at mealtimes.

The consort will not sit until the princess has been seated.

The consort will rise the moment the princess rises.

The consort will not engage in any sort of risk-taking behavior, such as racing—either car or boat—mountain-climbing, sky-diving, et cetera—until such time as an heir has been provided.

The consort will give up his right, in the event of annulment or divorce, to custody of any children born during the marriage.

The consort will give up the citizenship of his native country in favor of citizenship of Genovia.

Okay. Seriously. What kind of dweeb am I going to end up with?

Actually, I'll be lucky if I can get anybody to marry me at all. What schmuck would want to marry a girl he can't interrupt? Or can't walk out on during an argument? Or has to give up citizenship of his own country for?

I shudder to think of the total loser I will one day be forced to marry. I am already in mourning for the cool race car–driving, mountain-climbing, sky-diving guy I could have had, if it weren't for this whole crummy princess thing.

TOP FIVE WORST THINGS ABOUT BEING A PRINCESS

1. Can't marry Michael Moscovitz (he would never renounce his American citizenship in favor of Genovian).
2. Can't go anywhere without a bodyguard (I like Lars, but come on: Even the Pope gets to pray by himself sometimes).
3. Must maintain neutral opinion on important topics such as the meat industry and smoking.
4. Princess lessons with Grandmère.
5. Still forced to learn Algebra even though there is no reason why I will ever have to use it in my future career as ruler of small European principality.

Monday, October 27, Later

I figured as soon as I got home, I would tell my mom that she and Mr. G need to elope, and right away. Grandmère had brought in a professional! I knew it would be a pain, what with Mom's latest show opening being so soon and all, but it was either that, or a royal wedding the likes of which this city hasn't seen since . . .

Well, ever.

But when I got home, my mom had her head in the toilet.

It turns out her morning sickness has begun, and isn't at all exclusive. She'll throw up just about any time, not just in the a.m.

She was so sick, I didn't have the heart to make her feel worse by telling her what Grandmère had planned.

"Be sure to put a video in," my mom kept calling from the bathroom. I didn't know what she was talking about, but Mr. G did.

She meant to be sure to tape my interview. My interview with Beverly Bellerieve!

I had completely forgotten about it, in light of what had happened at Grandmère's. But my mom hadn't.

Since my mom was incapacitated, Mr. G and I settled in to watch my interview together—well, in between running into the bathroom to offer my mom seltzer and saltines.

I figured I would tell Mr. G about Grandmère and the wedding at the first commercial break—but I sort of forgot, in the unbelievable horror of what followed.

Beverly Bellerieve—undoubtedly in an effort to impress

my father—actually did messenger over both a videotape and a written transcript of the interview. I will enclose parts of the written transcript here, so if I am ever asked to do another interview again, I can look at it and know exactly why I should never allow myself to appear on television ever again.

TWENTYFOUR/SEVEN for Monday 27 October

America's Princess
B. Bellerieve int. w/M. Renaldo

Ext. Thompson Street, south of Houston (SoHo). World Trade in background.

Beverly Bellerieve (BB):

Imagine if you will, an ordinary teenage girl. Well, as ordinary as a teenage girl who lives in New York City's Greenwich Village with her single mom, acclaimed painter Helen Thermopolis, can be.

Mia's life was filled with the normal things most teenagers' lives are full of—homework, friends, and the occasional F in Algebra . . . until one day, it all changed.

Int. penthouse suite, Plaza Hotel.

BB: Mia—may I call you Mia? Or would you prefer that I call you Your Highness? Or Amelia?

Mia Renaldo (MR):

Um, no, you can call me Mia.

BB: Mia. Tell us about that day. The day life as you know it changed completely.

MR: Well, um, what happened was, my dad and I were here

at the Plaza, you know, and I was drinking tea, and I got the hiccups, and everyone was looking at me, and my dad was, you know, trying to tell me I was the heir to the throne of Genovia, the country where he lives, and I was like, Look, I gotta go to the bathroom, and so I did, and I waited there until my hiccups stopped and then I came back to my chair and he told me that I was a princess and I completely flipped out and I ran to the zoo and I sat and looked at the penguins for a while and I totally couldn't believe it because in the seventh grade they made us do fact sheets on all the countries in Europe, but I totally missed the part about my dad being prince of it. And all I could think was that I was going to die if people in school found out, because I didn't want to end up being a freak like my friend Tina, who has to go around school with a body-guard. But that's exactly what happened. I am a freak, a huge freak.

[This is the part where she tries to salvage the situation:]

BB: Oh, Mia, I can't believe that's true. I'm sure you're quite popular.

MR: No, I'm not. I'm not popular at all. Only jocks are popular in my school. And cheerleaders. But I'm not popular. I mean, I don't hang out with the popular people. I never get invited to parties, or anything. I mean, the cool parties, where there is beer and making out and stuff. I mean, I'm not a jock, or a cheerleader, or one of the smart kids—

BB: Oh, but aren't you one of the smart kids, though? I understand one of your classes is called Gifted and Talented.

MR: Yes, but see, G and T is just like study hall. We don't

actually do anything in this class. Except goof around because the teacher is never there, she's always in the teachers' lounge across the hall so she has no idea what we're doing. Which is goofing off.

[Obviously still thinking she can make something out of this interview:]

BB: But I don't imagine you have much time for goofing off, do you, Mia? For instance, we are sitting here in the penthouse suite that belongs to your grandmother, the celebrated dowager princess of Genovia, who is, I understand, instructing you in royal decorum.

MR: Oh, yes. She's giving me princess lessons after school. Well, after my Algebra review sessions, which are after school.

BB: Mia, didn't you have some exciting news recently?

MR: Oh. Yes. Well, I'm pretty excited. I've always wanted to be a big sister. But they don't really want to make a big deal out of it, you know. It's just going to be a very small ceremony at City Hall—

There's more. A lot more, actually. It's too excruciating to go into. Basically, I just babbled like an idiot for about another ten minutes, while Beverly Bellerieve frantically attempted to steer me back toward something resembling the actual question she'd asked me.

But it was completely beyond even her impressive journalistic abilities. I was gone. A combination of nerves and, I'm afraid to say, codeine cough syrup, put me over the edge.

Ms. Bellerieve tried, though. I have to give her that. The interview ended with this:

Ext. Thompson Street, SoHo.

BB: She's not a jock, nor is she a cheerleader. What Amelia Mignonette Grimaldi Thermopolis Renaldo is, ladies and gentlemen, defies the societal stereotypes that exist in today's modern educational institutions. She's a princess. An American princess.

Yet she faces the same problems and pressures that teenagers all over this country face every day. . . with a twist: One day, she'll grow up to govern a nation.

And come spring, she'll be a big sister. Yes, *TwentyFour/Seven* has discovered that Helen Thermopolis and Mia's Algebra teacher, Frank Gianini—who are unmarried—are expecting their first child in May. When we come back, an exclusive interview with Mia's father, the prince of Genovia . . . next on *TwentyFour/Seven.*

What it all boiled down to is that, basically, I'm moving to Genovia.

My mom, who finally came out toward the end of the tape, and Mr. G tried to convince me that it wasn't that bad.

But it was. Oh, believe me, it was.

And I knew I was in for it the minute the phone started ringing, right after the segment aired.

"Oh God," my mother said, suddenly remembering something. "Don't pick it up! It's my mother! Frank, I forgot to tell my mother about us!"

Actually, I was kind of hoping it was Grandma

Thermopolis. Grandma Thermopolis was infinitely prefer-able, in my opinion, to who it actually turned out to be: Lilly.

And boy, was she mad.

"What do you mean, calling us a bunch of freaks?" she screamed into the phone.

I said, "Lilly, what are you talking about? I didn't call you a freak."

"You basically informed the entire nation that the popu-lation of Albert Einstein High School is divided into vari-ous socioeconomic cliques, and that you and your friends are too uncool to be in any of them!"

"Well," I said. "We are."

"Speak for yourself! And what about G and T?"

"What *about* G and T?"

"You just told the entire country that we sit in there and goof off because Mrs. Hill is always in the teachers' lounge! What are you, stupid? You've probably gotten her into trouble!"

I felt something inside of me clench, as if someone was squeezing my intestines very, very tightly.

"Oh, no," I breathed. "Do you really think so?"

Lilly just let out a frustrated scream, then snarled, "My parents say to tell your mother mazel tov."

Then she slammed the phone down.

I felt worse than ever. Poor Mrs. Hill!

Then the phone rang again. It was Shameeka.

"Mia," she said. "Remember how I invited you to my Halloween party this Friday?"

"Yes," I said.

"Well, my dad won't let me have it now."

"*What?* Why?"

"Because thanks to you he is under the impression that Albert Einstein High School is filled with sex addicts and alcoholics."

"But I didn't say that!" Not in those exact words, anyway.

"Well, that's what he heard. He is currently in the next room surfing the Internet for a girls' school in New Hampshire he can send me to next semester. And he says he's not letting me go out with a boy again until I'm thirty."

"Oh, Shameeka," I said. "I'm so sorry."

Shameeka didn't say anything. In fact, she had to hang up, because she was sobbing too hard to speak.

The phone rang again. I didn't want to answer it, but I had no choice: Mr. Gianini was holding my mom's hair back while she threw up some more.

"Hello?"

It was Tina Hakim Baba.

"Oh, my gosh!" she shouted.

"I'm sorry, Tina," I said, figuring I better just start apologizing to every single person who called, right off the bat.

"Sorry? What are you sorry for?" Tina was practically hyperventilating. "You said my name on TV!"

"Um . . . I know." I had also called her a freak.

"I can't believe it!" Tina yelled. "That was so cool!"

"You aren't . . . you aren't mad at me?"

"Why should I be mad at you? This is the most exciting thing that has ever happened to me. I've never had my name said on television before!"

I was filled with love and appreciation for Tina Hakim Baba.

"Um," I asked, carefully, "did your parents see it?"

"Yes! They're excited, too. My mom said to tell you that the blue eyeshadow was a stroke of genius. Not too much, just enough to catch the light. She was very impressed. Also she said to tell your mother she has some excellent stretch mark cream that she got in Sweden. You know, for when she starts getting big. I'll bring it to school tomorrow, and you can give it to your mother."

"What about your dad?" I asked, carefully. "He's not planning on sending you to girls' school or anything?"

"What are you talking about? He's delighted that you mentioned my bodyguard. Now he thinks anyone who'd had plans to kidnap me will definitely think twice. Oops, there's another call. It's probably my grandmother in Dubai. They have a satellite dish. I'm sure she heard you mention me! 'Bye!"

Tina hung up. Great. Even people in Dubai saw my interview. I don't even know where Dubai is.

The phone rang again. It was Grandmère.

"Well," she said. "That was just terrible, wasn't it?"

I said, "Is there any way I can demand a retraction? Because I didn't mean to say that my Gifted and Talented teacher doesn't do anything and that my school was full of sex addicts. It's not, you know."

"I cannot imagine what that woman was thinking," Grandmère said. I was pleased she was on my side for once. Then she went on, and I saw that she wasn't talking about anything to do with me. "She failed to show a single picture of the palace! And it is at its most beautiful in the autumn. The palm trees look magnificent. This is a travesty, I tell you.

A travesty. Do you realize the promotional opportunities that have been wasted here? Absolutely wasted?"

"Grandmère, you have to do something," I wailed. "I don't know if I'm going to be able to show my face at school tomorrow."

"Tourism has been down in Genovia," Grandmère reminded me, "ever since we banned cruise ships from docking in the bay. But who needs day-trippers? With their sticky-film cameras and their awful Bermuda shorts. If that woman had only shown a few shots of the casinos. And the beaches! Why, we have the only naturally white sand along the Riviera. Are you aware of that, Amelia? Monaco has to import their sand."

"Maybe I could transfer to another school. Do you think there's a school in Manhattan that will take someone with a one point zero in Algebra?"

"Wait—" Grandmère's voice became muffled. "Oh, no, there we are. It's back on, and they're showing some simply lovely shots of the palace. Oh, and there's the beach. And the bay. Oh, and the olive groves. Lovely. Simply lovely. That woman might have a few redeeming qualities after all. I suppose I will have to allow your father to continue seeing her."

She hung up. My own grandmother hung up on me. What kind of a reject am I, anyway?

I went into my mom's bathroom. She was sitting on the floor, looking unhappy. Mr. Gianini was sitting on the edge of the bathtub. He looked confused.

Well, who can blame him? A couple of months ago, he was just an Algebra teacher. Now he's the father of the future sibling of the princess of Genovia.

"I need to find another school to go to from now on," I informed them. "Do you think you could help me out with that, Mr. G? I mean, do you have any pull with the teachers' association, or anything?"

My mother went, "Oh, Mia. It wasn't that bad."

"Yes, it was," I said. "You didn't even see most of it. You were in here throwing up."

"Yes," my mother said. "But I could hear it. And what did you say that wasn't true? People who excel at sports have traditionally been treated like gods in our society, while people whose brilliance is cerebral are routinely ignored, or worse, mocked as nerds or geeks. Frankly, I believe scientists working on cures for cancer should be paid the salaries professional athletes are receiving. Professional athletes aren't out there saving lives, for God's sake. They entertain. And actors. Don't tell me acting is art. Teaching. Now there's an art. Frank should be making what Tom Cruise does, for teaching you how to multiply fractions the way he did."

I realized my mother was probably delusional with nausea. I said, "Well, I think I'll just be going to bed now."

Instead of replying, my mother leaned over the toilet and threw up some more. I could see that in spite of all my warnings about the potential lethality of shellfish for a developing fetus, she'd ordered jumbo prawns in garlic sauce from Number One Noodle Son.

I went to my room and went online. Maybe, I thought, I could transfer to the same school Shameeka's father is shipping her off to. At least then I'd already have one friend—if Shameeka would even speak to me after what I'd done, which I doubted. No one at Albert Einstein High, with the exception of Tina Hakim Baba, who was obviously clueless, was ever going to speak to me again.

Then an instant message flashed across my computer screen. Someone wanted to talk to me.

But who? Jo-C-rox??? Was it Jo-C-rox?????

No. Even better! It was Michael. Michael, at least, still wanted to talk to me.

I have printed out our conversation and stuck it here:

CRACKING: Hey. Just saw you on TV. You were good.

FTLOUIE: What are you talking about? I made a complete and utter fool of myself. And what about Mrs. Hill? They're probably going to fire her now.

CRACKING: Well, at least you told the truth.

FTLOUIE: But all these people are mad at me now! Lilly's furious!

CRACKING: She's just jealous because you had more people watching you in that one fifteen-minute segment than all the people who've ever watched all of her shows put together.

FTLOUIE: No, that's not why. She thinks I've betrayed our generation, or something, by revealing that cliques exist at Albert Einstein High School.

CRACKING: Well, that, and the fact that you claimed you don't belong to any of them.

FTLOUIE: Well, I don't.

CRACKING: Yes, you do. Lilly likes to think you belong to the exclusive and highly selective Lilly Moscovitz clique. Only you neglected to mention this, and that has upset her.

FTLOUIE: Really? Did she say that?

CRACKING: She didn't say it, but she's my sister. I know

the way she thinks.

FTLOUIE: Maybe. I don't know, Michael.

CRACKING: Look, are you all right? You were a mess at school today ... although now it's clear why. That's pretty cool about your mom and Mr. Gianini. You must be excited.

FTLOUIE: I guess so. I mean, it's kind of embarrassing. But at least this time my mom's getting married, like a normal person.

CRACKING: Now you won't need my help with your Algebra homework anymore. You'll have your own personal tutor right there at home.

I had never thought of this. How awful! I don't want my own personal tutor. I want Michael to keep helping me during G and T! Mr. Gianini is all right, and everything, but he's certainly not *Michael*.

I wrote really fast:

FTLOUIE: Well, I don't know. I mean, he's going to be awfully busy for a while, moving in, and then there'll be the baby and everything.

CRACKING: God. A baby. I can't believe it. No wonder you were wigging out so badly today.

FTLOUIE: Yeah, I really was. Wigging out, I mean.

CRACKING: And what about that thing this afternoon with Lana? That couldn't have helped much. Though it was pretty funny, her thinking we were going out, huh?

Actually, I didn't see anything particularly funny about it. But what was I supposed to say? Gee, Michael, why don't we give it a try?

As if.

Instead I said:

FTLOUIE: Yeah, she's such a headcase. I guess it's never occurred to her that two people of the opposite sex can just be friends, with no romantic involvement.

Although I have to admit the way I feel about Michael—particularly when I'm over at Lilly's and he comes out of his room with no shirt on—is quite romantic.

CRACKING: Yeah. Listen, what are you doing Friday night?

Was he asking me out? Was Michael Moscovitz finally asking me OUT?

No. It wasn't possible. Not after the way I'd made a fool of myself on national television.

Just to be safe, though, I figured I'd try for a neutral reply, in case what he wanted to know was whether I could come over and walk Pavlov because the Moscovitzes were going to be out of town, or something.

FTLOUIE: I don't know. Why?

CRACKING: Because it's Halloween, you know. I thought a bunch of us could get together and go see *The Rocky Horror Picture Show* over at the Village Cinema. . . .

Okay. Not a date.

But we'd be sitting beside each other in a darkened

room! That counted for something. And *Rocky Horror* is sort of scary, so if I reached over and grabbed him, it might be okay.

FtLouie: Sure, that sounds . . .

Then I remembered. Friday night was Halloween, all right. But it was also the night of my mom's royal wedding! I mean, if Grandmère gets her way.

FtLouie: Can I get back to you? I may have a family obligation that evening.
CracKing: Sure. Just let me know. Well, see you tomorrow.
FtLouie: Yeah. I can't wait.
CracKing: Don't worry. You were telling the truth. You can't get in trouble for telling the truth.

Ha! That's what he thinks. There's a reason I lie all the time, you know.

TOP FIVE BEST THINGS ABOUT BEING IN LOVE WITH YOUR BEST FRIEND'S BROTHER

1. Get to see him in his natural environment, not just at school, thus allowing you access to vital information, like difference between his "school" personality and real personality.
2. Get to see him without a shirt on.
3. Get to see him all the time.
4. Get to see how he treats his mother/sister/ housekeeper (critical clues as to how he will treat any prospective girlfriend).
5. Convenient: You can hang out with your friend and spy on the object of your affections at the same time.

TOP FIVE WORST THINGS ABOUT BEING IN LOVE WITH YOUR BEST FRIEND'S BROTHER

1. Can't tell her.
2. Can't tell him, because he might tell her.
3. Can't tell anyone else, because they might tell him, or worse, her.
4. He will never admit to his true feelings because you are his little sister's best friend.
5. You are continuously thrust into his presence, knowing that he will never think of you as anything but his little sister's best friend for as long as you live, and yet you continue to pine for him until every fiber of your being cries out for him and you think you are probably going to die even though your Biology teacher says it is physiologically impossible to die from a broken heart.

Oh, God! No sooner had I set foot in Homeroom today than I was summoned to the principal's office!

I was hoping it was so that she could make sure I'm not carrying any contraband cough syrup, but it's more likely because of what I said last night on TV. Particularly, I would guess, the part about how divisive and clique-ridden it is around here.

Meanwhile, all the other people in this school who have never been invited to a party given by a popular kid have rallied around me. It's like I've struck a blow for dweebs everywhere, or something. The minute I walked into school today, the hip-hoppers, the brainiacs, the drama freaks, they were all, "Hey! Tell it like it is, sistah."

No one's ever called me sistah before. It is somewhat invigorating.

Only the cheerleaders treat me the way they always have. As I walk down the hall, their eyes flick over me, from the top of my head all the way down to my shoes. And then they whisper to each other and laugh.

Well, I suppose it is amusing to see a five-foot-nine, flat-chested amazon like myself roaming loose in the halls. I'm surprised no one has thrown a net over me and hauled me off to the Natural History Museum.

Of my own friends, only Lilly—and Shameeka, of course—aren't entirely thrilled with last night's performance. Lilly's still unhappy about my spilling the beans about the socioeconomic division of our school population. Not unhappy enough to turn down a ride to school in my limo this morning, however.

Interestingly, Lilly's chilly treatment of me has only served to bring her brother and I closer. This morning in the limo on the way to school, Michael offered to go over my Algebra homework with me, and make sure my equations were all right.

I was touched by his offer, and the warm feeling I had when he pronounced all my problems correct didn't have anything to do with pride, but everything to do with the way his fingers brushed against mine as he handed the piece of paper back to me. Could he be Jo-C-rox? *Could he?*

Uh-oh. Principal Gupta is ready to see me now.

Tuesday, October 28, Algebra

Principal Gupta is way concerned about my mental health.

"Mia, are you really so unhappy here at Albert Einstein?"

I didn't want to hurt her feelings or anything, so I said no. I mean, the truth is, it probably wouldn't matter what school somebody stuck me in. I will always be a five-foot-nine freak with no breasts, no matter where I go.

Then Principal Gupta said something surprising: "I only ask because last night during your interview, you said you weren't popular."

I wasn't quite sure where she was going with this. So I just said, "Well, I'm not," with a shrug.

"That isn't true," Principal Gupta said. "Everyone in the school knows who you are."

I still didn't want her to feel bad, like it was her fault I'm a biological sport, so I explained very gently, "Yes, but that's only because I'm a princess. Before that, I was pretty much invisible."

Principal Gupta said, "That simply isn't true."

But all I could think was, *How would you even know? You aren't out there. You don't know what it's like.*

And then I felt even worse for her, because she is so obviously living in principal fantasy world.

"Perhaps," Principal Gupta said, "if you took part in more extracurricular activities, you'd feel a better sense of belonging."

This caused my jaw to drop.

"Principal Gupta," I couldn't help exclaiming. "I am

barely passing Algebra. All of my free time is spent attending review sessions so that I can scrape by with a D."

"Well," Principal Gupta said, "I am aware of that—"

"Also, after my review sessions, I have princess lessons with my grandmother, so that when I go to Genovia in December for my introduction to the people I will one day rule, I do not make a complete idiot of myself, like I did last night on TV."

"I think the word *idiot* might be a little strong."

"I really don't have time," I went on, feeling more sorry for her than ever, "for extracurricular activities."

"The yearbook committee meets only once a week," Principal Gupta said. "Or perhaps you could join the track team. They won't begin training until the spring, and by that time, hopefully, you won't be having princess lessons anymore."

I just blinked at her, I was so surprised. *Me? Track?* I can barely walk without tripping over my own gargantuan feet. God knows what would happen if I tried running.

And the yearbook committee? Did I really look like someone who wants to remember one single thing about my high school experience?

"Well," Principal Gupta said, I guess realizing from my facial expression that I was not enthused by either of these suggestions. "It was just an idea. I do think you would be much happier here at Albert Einstein if you joined a club. I am aware, of course, of your friendship with Lilly Moscovitz, and I sometimes wonder if she might not be . . . well, a negative influence on you. That television show of hers is quite acerbic."

I was shocked by this. Poor Principal Gupta is more deluded than I thought!

"Oh, no," I said. "Lilly's show is actually quite positive. Didn't you see the episode dedicated to fighting racism in Korean delis? Or the one about how a lot of clothing stores that cater to teens are prejudiced against larger-size girls, since they don't carry enough things in size twelve, the size of the average American woman? Or the one where we tried to hand-deliver a pound of Vaniero cookies to Freddie Prinz Jr.'s apartment because he'd been looking a little thin?"

Principal Gupta held up her hand. "I see that you feel very passionately about this," she said. "And I must say, I am pleased. It is good to know you feel passionate about something, Mia, other than your antipathy toward athletes and cheerleaders."

Then I felt worse than ever. I said, "I don't feel antipathy toward them. I'm just saying that sometimes . . . well, sometimes it feels like they run this school, Principal Gupta."

"Well, I can assure you," Principal Gupta said. "That is not true."

Poor, poor Principal Gupta.

Still, I did feel that I had to intrude upon the fantasy world in which she so obviously lives, just a little.

"Um," I said. "Principal Gupta. About Mrs. Hill . . ."

"What about her?" Principal Gupta asked.

"I didn't mean it when I said she's always in the teachers' lounge during my Gifted and Talented class. That was an exaggeration."

Principal Gupta smiled at me in this very brittle way.

"Don't worry, Mia," she said. "Mrs. Hill has been taken care of."

Taken care of! What does *that* mean?

I am almost scared to find out.

Well, Mrs. Hill didn't get fired.

Instead, I guess they gave her a warning, or something. The upshot of it is, Mrs. Hill won't budge from behind her desk here in the G and T lab.

Which means we have to sit at our desks and actually do our work. And we can't lock Boris in the supply closet. We actually have to sit here and listen to him play.

Play *Bartok*.

And we can't talk to one another, because we are supposed to be working on our individual projects.

Boy, is everyone mad at me.

But no one is madder than Lilly.

It turns out Lilly's been secretly writing a book about the socioeconomic divisions that exist within the walls of Albert Einstein High School. Really! She didn't want to tell me, but finally Boris blurted it out at lunch today. Lilly threw a fry at him and got ketchup all over his sweater.

I can't believe Lilly has told Boris things that she hasn't told me. I'm supposed to be her best friend. Boris is just her boyfriend. Why is she telling him cool things, like about how she's writing a book, and not telling me?

"Can I read it?" I begged.

"No." Lilly was really mad. She wouldn't even look at Boris. He had already totally forgiven her about the ketchup, even though he will probably have to get that sweater dry-cleaned.

"Can I read just one page?" I asked.

"No."

"Just one sentence?"

"No."

Michael didn't know about the book either. He told me right before Mrs. Hill came in that he offered to publish it in his webzine, *Crackhead*, but Lilly said, in quite a snotty voice, that she was holding out for a "legitimate" publisher.

"Am I in it?" I wanted to know. "Your book? Am I in it?"

Lilly said if people don't stop bothering her about it, she is going to fling herself off the top of the school water tower. She is exaggerating, of course. You can't even get up to the water tower anymore, since the seniors, as a prank a few years ago, poured a bunch of tadpoles into it.

I can't believe Lilly's been working on a book and never told me. I mean, I always knew she was going to write a book about the adolescent experience in post–Cold War America. But I didn't think she was going to start it before we had graduated. If you ask me, this book can't be very balanced. Because I hear things get way better sophomore year.

Still, I guess it does make sense that you would tell someone whose tongue has been in your mouth things you wouldn't necessarily tell your best friend. But it makes me mad Boris knows things about Lilly that I don't know. I tell Lilly everything.

Well, everything except how I feel about her brother.

Oh, and about my secret admirer.

And about my mom and Mr. Gianini.

But I tell her practically everything else.

DON'T FORGET:

1. Stop thinking about M.M.
2. English journal! Profound moment!
3. Cat food
4. Q-tips
5. Toothpaste
6. TOILET PAPER!

I am winning friends and influencing people everywhere I go today. Kenny just asked me what I'm doing for Halloween. I said I might have a family obligation to attend, and he said if I could get out of it, he and a bunch of his friends from the Computer Club are going to *Rocky Horror*, and that I should come along.

I asked him if one of his friends was Michael Moscovitz, because Michael is treasurer of the Computer Club, and he said yes.

I thought about asking Kenny if he's heard Michael mention whether or not he likes me, you know, in any special way, but I decided not to.

Because then Kenny might think I like him. Michael, I mean. And how pathetic would I look *then*?

Ode to M

Oh, M,
why can't you see
that x = you
and y = me?
And that
you + me
 = ecstasy,
and together we'd B
4ever happy?

What with all the backlash about my interview on *TwentyFour/Seven*, I completely forgot about Grandmère and Vigo, the Genovian event organizer!

I mean it. I swear I didn't remember a thing about Vigo and the asparagus tips, not until I walked into Grandmère's suite tonight for my princess lesson, and there were all these people scurrying around, doing things like barking into the phone: "No, that's four *thousand* long-stemmed pink roses, not four *hundred*," and calligraphy-ing place cards.

I found Grandmère sitting in the midst of all this activity, sampling truffles with Rommel—stylishly dressed in a chinchilla cape, dyed mauve—in her lap.

I'm not kidding. Truffles.

"No," Grandmère said, putting a gooey half-eaten chocolate ball back into the box Vigo was holding out to her. "Not that one, I think. Cherries are so *vulgar*."

"Grandmère." I couldn't believe this. I was practically hyperventilating, the way Grandmère had when she'd found out my mom was pregnant. "What are you *doing*? Who are all these people?"

"Ah, Mia," Grandmère said, looking pleased to see me. Even though, judging from the remains in the box Vigo was holding, she'd been eating a lot of stuff with nougat in it, none of it got onto her teeth. This is one of the many royal tricks Grandmère had yet to teach me. "Lovely. Sit down and help me decide which of these truffles we should put in the gift box the wedding guests are getting as party favors."

"Wedding guests?" I sank onto the chair Vigo had pulled up for me, and dropped my backpack. "Grandmère, I told you. My mom is never going to go along with this. She wouldn't *want* something like this."

Grandmère just shook her head and said, "Pregnant women are never the most rational creatures."

I pointed out that, judging from my research into the matter, while it was true that hormonal imbalances often cause pregnant women discomfort, I saw no reason to suppose that these imbalances in any way invalidated my mother's feelings on the matter—especially since I knew that they'd have been exactly the same if she weren't pregnant. My mom is not a royal wedding type of gal. I mean, she gets together with her girlfriends for margarita-poker night once a month.

"She," Vigo pointed out, "is the mother of the future reigning monarch of Genovia, Your Highness. As such, it is vital that she be extended every privilege and courtesy the palace can offer."

"Then how about offering her the privilege of planning her wedding for herself?" I said.

Grandmère had a good laugh at that one. She practically choked on the swig of Sidecar she was taking after each bite of truffle in order to cleanse her palate.

"Amelia," she said, when she was through coughing—something Rommel had found extremely alarming, if the way he rolled his eyes back up into his head was any indication. "Your mother will be eternally grateful to us for all the work we are doing on her behalf. You'll see."

I realized it was no good arguing with them. I knew what

I was going to have to do.

And I would do it right after my lesson, which was how to write a royal thank-you note. You would not believe all the wedding presents and baby stuff that people have started sending my mother, care of the Genovian royal family at the Plaza Hotel. Seriously. It is unreal. The place is jam-packed with electric woks, waffle irons, tablecloths, baby shoes, baby hats, baby clothes, baby diapers, baby toys, baby swings, baby changing tables, baby you-name-it. I had no idea so much stuff was necessary for raising a baby. But I have a pretty good idea my mom isn't going to want any of it. She's not really into pastels.

I marched up to the door to my father's hotel suite, and banged on it.

He wasn't there! And when I asked the concierge down in the lobby if she knew where my dad had gone, she said she wasn't sure.

One thing she was quite certain of, however, was that Beverly Bellerieve had been with my dad when he'd left.

Well, I'm glad my dad's found a new friend, I guess, but hello? Is he not aware of the impending disaster growing under his own royal nose?

Well, it happened. The impending disaster is now officially a *real* disaster.

Because Grandmère has gotten completely out of hand. I didn't even realize how badly, either, until I got home tonight from my lesson and saw this *family* sitting at our dining-room table.

That's right. An entire *family*. Well, a mom and a dad and a kid, anyway.

I am not kidding. At first I thought they were tourists that had maybe taken a wrong turn—our neighborhood is very touristy. Like maybe they thought they were going to Washington Square Park, but ended up following a Chinese food delivery guy to our loft instead.

But then the woman who was wearing pink jogging pants—a clear indication that she was from out of town—looked at me and said, "Oh, my Lord! Are you telling me that you actually wear your hair like that in real life? I was sure it was just that way for TV."

My jaw dropped. I went, "*Grandmother Thermopolis?*"

"Grandmother Thermopolis?" The woman squinted at me. "I guess all this royal stuff really *has* gone to your head. Don't you remember me, honey? I'm *Mamaw*."

Mamaw! My grandmother from my mother's side!

And there, sitting beside her—roughly half her size and wearing a baseball cap—was my mother's father, Papaw! The hulking boy in a flannel shirt and overalls I didn't recognize, but that hardly mattered. What were my mother's estranged parents, who had never left Versailles,

Indiana, before in their lives, doing in our downtown Village loft?

A quick consultation with my mother explained it. I was able to find her by following the phone cord first into her bedroom, then into her walk-in closet, where she was huddled behind her shoe rack (empty—all her shoes were on the floor) in whispered conspiracy with my father.

"I don't care how you do it, Phillipe," she was hissing into the phone. "You tell that mother of yours she's gone too far this time. My *parents*, Phillipe? *You know how I feel about my parents.* If you don't get them out of here, Mia is going to end up paying visits to me through a slot in the door up at Bellevue."

I could hear my father murmuring reassurances through the phone. My mom noticed me and whispered, "Are they still out there?"

I said, "Um, yes. You mean you didn't invite them?"

"Of course not!" My mother's eyes were as wide as Calamata olives. "Your grandmother invited them for some cockamamie wedding she thinks she's throwing for me and Frank on Friday!"

I gulped guiltily. Oops.

Well, all I can say in my own defense is that things have been very very hectic lately. I mean, what with finding out my mother is pregnant, and then getting sick, and the whole thing with Jo-C-rox, and then the interview. . . .

Oh, all right. There's no excuse. I am a horrible daughter.

My mom held out the phone to me. "He wants to talk to you," she said.

I took the phone and went, "Dad? Where are you?"

"I'm in the car," he said. "Listen, Mia, I got the concierge to arrange for rooms for your grandparents at a hotel near your place—the SoHo Grand. Okay? Just put them in the limo and send them there."

"Okay, Dad," I said. "What about Grandmère and this whole wedding thing? I mean, it's sort of out of control." Understatement of the year.

"I'll take care of Grandmère," my dad said, sounding very Captain Picardish. You know, from *Star Trek: The Next Generation*. I got the feeling Beverly Bellerieve was there in the car with him, and he was trying to sound all princely in front of her.

"Okay," I said. "But . . ."

It's not that I didn't trust my dad, or anything, to take care of the situation. It's just—well, we are talking about Grandmère. She can be very scary, when she wants to be. Even, I am sure, to her own son.

I guess he must have known what I was thinking, since he said, "Don't worry, Mia. I'll take care of it."

"Okay," I said, feeling bad for doubting him.

"And Mia?"

I'd been about to hang up. "Yeah, Dad?"

"Assure your mother I didn't know anything about this. I *swear* it."

"Okay, Dad."

I hung up the phone. "Don't worry," I said to my mom. "I'll take care of this."

Then, my shoulders back, I returned to the living room. My grandparents were still sitting at the table. Their farmer friend, however, had gotten up. He was in the kitchen, peering into the refrigerator.

"This all you got to eat around here?" he asked, pointing to the carton of soy milk and the bowl of edamame on the first shelf.

"Um," I said. "Well, yes. We are trying to keep our refrigerator free from any sort of contaminants that might harm a developing fetus."

When the guy looked blank, I said, "We usually order in."

He brightened at once, and closed the refrigerator door. "Oh, Dominos?" he said. "Great!"

"Um," I said. "Well, you can order Dominos, if you want, from your hotel room—"

"Hotel room?"

I spun around. Mamaw had snuck up behind me.

"Um, yes," I said. "You see, my father thought you might be more comfortable at a nice hotel than here in the loft—"

"Well, if that doesn't beat all," Mamaw said. "Here your Papaw and Hank and I come all the way to see you, and you stick us in a hotel?"

I looked at the guy in the overalls with renewed interest. *Hank?* As in my *cousin* Hank? Why, the last time I'd seen Hank had been during my second—and ultimately final—trip to Versailles, back when I'd been about ten or so. Hank had been dropped off at the Thermopolis homestead the year before by his globe-trotting mother—my aunt Marie, who my mom can't stand, primarily because, as my mother puts it, she exists in an intellectual and spiritual vacuum (meaning that Marie is a Republican).

Back then, Hank had been a skinny, whiny thing with a

milk allergy. He wasn't as skinny as he'd once been, but he still looked a little lactose intolerant, if you ask me.

"Nobody said anything about us being hauled off to an expensive New York City hotel when that French woman called." Mamaw had followed me into the kitchen, and now she stood with her hands on her generous hips. "She said she'd pay for everything," Mamaw said, "free and clear."

I realized at once where Mamaw's concern lay.

"Oh, um, Mamaw," I said. "My father will take care of the bill, of course."

"Well, that's different." Mamaw beamed. "Let's go!"

I figured I'd better go with them, just to make sure they got there all right. As soon as we got into the limo, Hank forgot all about how hungry he was, in his delight over all the buttons there were to push. He had a swell time sticking his head in and out of the sun roof. At one point he stuck his whole body through the sun roof, spread his arms out wide, and yelled, "I'm the king of the world!"

Fortunately the limo's windows are tinted, so I don't think anyone from school could have recognized me, but I couldn't help feeling mortified.

So you can understand why, after I got them all checked into the hotel and everything, and Mamaw asked me if I would take Hank to school with me in the morning, I nearly passed out.

"Oh, you don't want to go to school with me, Hank," I said, quickly. "I mean, you're on vacation. You could go do something really fun." I tried to think of something that might seem really fun to Hank. "Like go to the Harley Davidson Cafe."

But Hank said, "Heck, no. I want to go to school with you, Mia. I always wanted to see what it was like at a real New York City high school." He lowered his voice, so Mamaw and Papaw wouldn't hear. "I hear the girls in New York City have all got their belly buttons pierced."

Hank was in for a real big disappointment if he thought he'd see any pierced navels in my school—we wear uniforms, and you aren't even allowed to tie the ends of your shirt into a halter top, a la Britney Spears.

But I couldn't see a way to get out of having him accompany me for the day. Grandmère was always going on about how princesses have to be gracious. Well, I guess this is my big test.

So I said, "Okay." Which didn't sound very gracious, but what else could I say?

Then Mamaw surprised me by grabbing me and giving me a hug good-bye. I don't know why I was so surprised. This was a very grandmotherly thing to do, of course. But I guess, seeing as how the grandmother I spend the most time with is Grandmère, I wasn't expecting it.

As she hugged me, Mamaw said, "Why, you aren't anything but skin and bones, are you?" Yes, thank you, Mamaw. It is true, I am mammarily challenged. But must you shout it out in the lobby of the SoHo Grand? "And when are you going to stop shooting up so high? I swear, you're almost taller than Hank!"

Which was, unfortunately, true.

Then Mamaw made Papaw give me a hug good-bye, too. Mamaw had been very soft when I hugged her. Papaw was the exact opposite, very bony. It was sort of amazing to me that these two people had managed to turn my strong-willed, independent-minded mother into such a gibbering mess. I mean, Grandmère used to lock my dad in the castle dungeon when he was a kid, and he wasn't half as resentful toward her as my mom was toward her parents.

On the other hand, my dad is in deep denial and suffers from classic Oedipal issues. At least according to Lilly.

When I got home, my mom had moved from the closet to her bed, where she lay covered with Victoria's Secret and J. Crew catalogs. I knew she must be feeling a little better. Ordering things is one of her favorite hobbies.

I said, "Hi, Mom."

She looked out from behind the Spring Bathing Suit edition. Her face was all bloated and splotchy. I was glad Mr. Gianini wasn't around. He might have had second thoughts about marrying her if he'd gotten a good look at her just then.

"Oh, Mia," she said when she saw me. "Come here and let me give you a hug. Was it horrible? I'm sorry I'm such a bad mother."

I sat down on the bed beside her. "You aren't a bad mother," I said. "You're a good mother. You just aren't feeling well."

"No," my mother said. She was sniffling, so I knew the reason she looked bloated and horrible was that she'd been crying. "I'm a terrible person. My parents came all the way from Indiana to see me, and I sent them to a hotel."

I could tell my mom was having a hormonal imbalance and wasn't herself. If she'd been herself, she wouldn't have thought twice about sending her parents to a hotel. She has never forgiven them for

a) not supporting her decision to have me,
b) not approving of the way she was raising me, and
c) voting for George Bush Sr., as well as his son.

Hormonal imbalance or not, though, the truth is, my mother does not need this kind of stress. This should be a really happy time for her. It says in all the stuff I've read about pregnancy that preparing for the birth of your child should be a time of joy and celebration.

And it would be, if Grandmère hadn't come around and ruined it all by sticking her nose where no one wants it.

She has *got* to be stopped.

And I'm not just saying that on account of how much I really, really want to go to *Rocky Horror* on Friday with Michael.

Tuesday, October 28, 11 p.m.

Another e-mail from Jo-C-rox!
This one said:

JoCrox: Dear Mia,
Just a note to tell you I saw you last night on TV. You looked
beautiful, as always. I know some people at school have been
giving you a hard time. Don't let them get you down. The
majority of us think you rock the world.
Your Friend

Isn't that the sweetest? I wrote back right away:

FtLouie: Dear Friend,
Thank you so much. PLEASE won't you tell me who you
are? I swear I won't tell a soul!!!!!!!!!!!!
Mia

He hasn't written back yet, but I think my sincerity really
shows, considering all the exclamation points.

I am slowly wearing him down, I just know it.

ENGLISH JOURNAL

My most profound moment was

ENGLISH JOURNAL

Make the most of yourself, for that is all there is of you.
                                    —Ralph Waldo Emerson

I believe that Mr. Emerson was talking about the fact that you are only given one life to live, and so you had better make the best of it. This idea is best illustrated by a movie I saw on the Lifetime Channel while I was sick. The movie was called *Who Is Julia?* In this movie, Mare Winningham portrays Julia, a woman who wakes up one day after an accident to discover that her body has been completely destroyed and her brain transplanted into someone whose body was okay but whose brain had ceased functioning. Since Julia formerly was a fashion model and now her brain is in a housewife's body (Mare Winningham's), she is understandably upset. She goes around banging her head against things because she is no longer blond, five foot ten, and a hundred and ten pounds.

But finally, through Julia's husband's undying devotion to her—despite her iffy new looks and a brief kidnapping by the housewife's psychotic husband, who wants her to come back home to do his laundry—Julia realizes that looking like a model isn't as important as not being dead.

This movie raises the inevitable question, If your body was destroyed in an accident, and they had to transplant your brain into someone else's body, whose body would you want it to be? After considerable thought, I have decided that I would most want to be in the body of Michelle Kwan, the Olympic ice skater, since she is very pretty and has a marketable skill. And as everyone knows, it is quite stylish these days to be Asian.

Either Michelle or Britney Spears, so I could finally have bigger breasts.

Well, one thing is for sure:

Having a guy like my cousin Hank follow you around from class to class certainly keeps people's minds off the idiot you made of yourself on TV the other night.

Seriously. Not that the cheerleaders have forgotten all about the whole *TwentyFour/Seven* thing—I'm still getting the evil eye in the hallway every once in a while. But as soon as their gazes flicked over me and settled on Hank, something seemed to happen to them.

I couldn't figure out what it was, at first. I thought it was just that they were so stunned to see a guy in a flannel shirt and overalls in the middle of Manhattan.

Then I slowly started realizing it was something else. I guess Hank is sort of buff, and he does have sort of nice blond hair that kind of hangs in his pretty-boy-blue eyes.

But I think it's something even more than that. It's like Hank is giving off those pheromones we studied in Bio, or something.

Only I can't sense them, because I am related to him.

As soon as girls notice Hank, they sidle up to me and whisper "Who is *that?*" while gazing longingly at Hank's biceps, which are actually quite pronounced beneath all that plaid.

Take Lana Weinberger, for instance. There she was, hanging around my locker, waiting for Josh to show up so the two of them could take part in their morning face-suckage ritual, when Hank and I appeared. Lana's eyes—heavily circled in Bobbi Brown—widened, and she went, "Who's your friend?" in this voice I had never heard her use before. And I've known her a while.

I said, "He's not my friend, he's my cousin."

Lana said to Hank, in the same strange voice, "You can be *my* friend."

To which Hank replied, with a big smile, "Gee, thanks, ma'am."

And don't think in Algebra Lana wasn't doing everything she could to get Hank to notice her. She swished her long blond hair all over my desk. She dropped her pencil like four times. She kept crossing and recrossing her legs. Finally Mr. Gianini was like, "Miss Weinberger, do you need a bathroom pass?" That calmed her down, but only for like five minutes.

Even Miss Molina, the school secretary, was strangely giggly when she was making out a guest pass for Hank.

But that's nothing compared to Lilly's reaction as she climbed into the limo this morning, when we swung by to pick up her and Michael. She looked across the seat and her jaw dropped open and this piece of Pop Tart she'd been chewing fell right out onto the floor. I'd never seen her do anything like that before in my life. Lilly is generally very good at keeping things in her mouth.

Hormones are very powerful things. We are helpless in their wake.

Which would certainly explain the whole Michael thing.

I mean, about my being so deeply besotted by him and all.

T. Hardy—buried his heart in Wessex, body in Westminster

Um, excuse me, but *gross*.

I don't believe this. I really don't.

Lilly and Hank are missing.

That's right. *Missing*.

Nobody knows where they are. Boris is beside himself. He won't stop playing Mahler. Even Mrs. Hill now agrees that shutting him into the supply closet is the best way to maintain our sanity. She let us sneak into the gymnasium and steal some exercise mats and lean them up against the supply closet door to muffle the sound.

It isn't working, though.

I guess I can understand Boris's despair. I mean, when you're a musical genius and the girl you've been French-kissing on a fairly regular basis suddenly disappears with a guy like Hank, it has to be demoralizing.

I should have seen it coming. Lilly was excessively flirty at lunch. She kept asking Hank all these questions about life back in Indiana. Like if he was the most popular boy in his school, and all. Which of course he said he was—though I personally don't believe being the most popular boy at Versailles (which in Indiana-speak is pronounced Ver-Sales, by the way) High School is such a big accomplishment.

Then she was all, "Do you have a girlfriend?"

Hank got bashful and said that he used to, only "Amber" had ditched him a couple weeks ago for a guy whose father owns the local Outback Steakhouse. Lilly acted all shocked, and said Amber must be suffering from a borderline personality disorder if she couldn't see what a fully self-actualized individual Hank was.

I was so revolted by this display, I could hardly keep my veggie burger down.

Then Lilly started talking about all the fabulous things there are to do in the city, and how Hank really ought to take advantage of them, rather than hanging around here at school with me. She said, "For instance, there's the Transit Museum, which is fascinating."

Seriously. She actually said the *Transit Museum* was fascinating. *Lilly Moscovitz.*

I swear, hormones are way dangerous.

Then she went, "And on Halloween, there's a parade in the Village, and then we are all going to *The Rocky Horror Picture Show*. Have you ever been to that before?"

Hank said that no, he hadn't.

I should have known right then that something was up, but I didn't. The bell rang, and Lilly said she wanted to take Hank to the auditorium to show him the part of the *My Fair Lady* set that she had painted herself (a street lamp). Feeling that even a momentary alleviation from Hank's constant stream of reminders of our last visit together—"Remember that time we left our bikes in the front yard and you were all worried somebody might come in the night and steal them?"—would be a relief, I said, "Okay."

And that was the last any of us saw of them.

I blame myself. Hank is apparently simply too attractive to be released amongst the general population. I ought to have recognized that. I ought to have recognized that the pull of an uneducated but completely gorgeous farm boy from Indiana would be stronger than the pull of a not-so-attractive musical genius from Russia.

Now I have turned my best friend into a two-timer AND a class ditcher. Lilly has never skipped a class in her life. If she gets caught, she will get detention. I wonder if she'll think sitting in the cafeteria for an hour after school with the other juvenile delinquents will be worth the fleeting moments of teenage lust she and Hank are sharing.

Michael is no help. He isn't worried about his sister at all. In fact, he seems to find the situation highly amusing. I have pointed out to him that for all we know, Lilly and Hank could have been kidnapped by Libyan terrorists, but he says he finds that unlikely. He thinks it more reasonable to assume that they are enjoying an afternoon showing at the Sony Imax.

As if. Hank is totally prone to motion sickness. He told us all about it when we drove past the cable car to Roosevelt Island this morning on the way to school.

What are Mamaw and Papaw going to say when they find out I lost their grandson?

TOP FIVE PLACES LILLY AND HANK
COULD BE
1. Transit Museum
2. Enjoying some corned beef at 2nd Avenue Deli
3. Looking up Dionysius Thermopolis's name on the wall of immigrants at Ellis Island
4. Getting tattoos on St. Marks' Place
5. Making wild passionate love back in his room at the SoHo Grand

OH, GOD!

Wednesday, October 29, World Civ

Still no sign of them.

Still nothing.

HOMEWORK

Algebra: solve problems #3, 9, 12 on pg. 147
English: Profound Moment!!!
World Civ: read Chapter 10
G&T: please
French: 4 sentences: une blague, la montagne, la mer,
il y a du soleil
Biology: ask Kenny

I am so sure—who can concentrate on homework when
your best friend and cousin are missing in New York
City????

Lars says he thinks it would be precipitous at this point to call the police. Mr. Gianini agrees with him. He says Lilly is ultimately quite sensible, and it is unrealistic to believe that she might let Hank fall into the hands of Libyan terrorists. I was, of course, only using Libyan terrorists as an example of the type of peril that might befall the two of them. There is another scenario which is much more disturbing:

Supposing Lilly is in love with him.

Seriously. Supposing Lilly, against all reason, has fallen madly in love with my cousin Hank, and he has fallen in love with her. Stranger things have happened. I mean, maybe Lilly is starting to realize that, yeah, Boris is a genius, but he still dresses funny and is incapable of breathing through his nose. Maybe she's willing to sacrifice those long intellectual conversations she and Boris used to have for a boy whose only asset is what is commonly referred to as booty.

And Hank, maybe he's been dazzled by Lilly's superior intellect. I mean, her IQ is easily a hundred points higher than his.

But can't they see that in spite of their mutual attraction, this relationship can only lead to ruin? I mean, suppose they DO IT, or something? And suppose that in spite of all those public service announcements on MTV, they neglect to practice safe sex, like my mom and Mr. G? They'll have to get married, and then Lilly will have to go live in Indiana in a trailer park, because that's where all teen mothers live. And she'll be wearing Wal-Mart housedresses and smoking

Kools while Hank goes off to the rubber tire factory and makes five fifty an hour.

Am I the only one who can see where all of this is heading? What is wrong with everyone?

First—grouping (evaluate with grouping symbols beginning with the innermost one)

Second—evaluate all powers

Third—multiply and divide left to right

Fourth—add and subtract in order left to right

It's all right. They're safe.

Apparently, Hank got back to the hotel around five, and Lilly showed up at her apartment, according to Michael, a little before that.

I would seriously like to know where they were, but all either of them will say is, "Just walking around."

Lilly adds, "God, could you be a little more possessive?"

I am so sure.

But I have bigger things to worry about. Right as I was about to step into Grandmère's suite at the Plaza for my princess lesson today, Dad appeared, looking nervous.

Only two things make my dad nervous. One is my mother.

And the other is his mother.

He said in a low voice, "Listen, Mia, about the wedding situation . . ."

I said, "I hope you had a chance to talk to Grandmère."

"Your grandmother has already sent out the invitations. To the wedding, I mean."

"*What?*"

Oh, my God. Oh, my God. This is a disaster. A *disaster*!

My dad must have known what I was thinking from my expression, since he went, "Mia, don't worry. I'll take care of it. Just leave it to me, all right?"

But how can I not worry? My dad is a good guy and all. At least he tries to be, anyway. But we're talking *Grandmère* here. *GRANDMÈRE*. Nobody goes up against Grandmère, not even the prince of Genovia.

And whatever he might have said to her so far, it certainly hasn't worked. She and Vigo are more deeply absorbed than ever in their nuptial planning.

"We have had acceptances already," Vigo informed me proudly when I walked in, "from the mayor, and Mr. Donald Trump, and Miss Diane Von Furstenberg, and the royal family of Sweden, and Mr. Oscar de la Renta, and Mr. John Tesh, and Miss Martha Stewart—"

I didn't say anything. That's because all I could think was what my mother was going to say if she walked down the aisle and there was John Tesh and Martha Stewart. She might actually run screaming from the room.

"Your dress arrived," Vigo informed me, his eyebrows waggling suggestively.

"My what?" I said.

Unfortunately Grandmère overheard me and clapped her hands so loudly she sent Rommel scurrying for cover, apparently thinking a nuclear missile or something had gone off.

"Do not ever let me hear you say *what* again," Grandmère fire-breathed at me. "Say, *I beg your pardon.*"

I looked at Vigo, who was trying not to smile. Really! Vigo actually thinks it's funny when Grandmère gets mad.

If there is a Genovian medal for valor, he should totally get it.

"I beg your pardon, Mr. Vigo," I said, politely.

"Please, please," Vigo said, waving his hand. "Just Vigo, none of this mister business, Your Highness. Now tell me. What do you think of this?"

And suddenly, he pulled this dress from a box.

And the minute I saw it, I was lost.

Because it was the most beautiful dress I have ever seen. It looked just like Glinda the Good Witch's dress from *The Wizard of Oz*—only not as sparkly. Still, it was pink, with this big poofy skirt, and it had little rosettes on the sleeves. I had never wanted a dress as much as I wanted that one the minute I laid eyes on it.

I had to try it on. I just had to.

Grandmère supervised the fitting, while Vigo hovered nearby, offering often to refresh her Sidecar. In addition to enjoying her favorite cocktail, Grandmère was smoking one of her long cigarettes, so she looked more officious than usual. She kept pointing with the cigarette and going, "No, not that way," and "For God's sake, stop slouching, Amelia."

It was determined that the dress was too big in the bust (what else is new?) and would have to be taken in. The alterations would take until Friday, but Vigo assured us he'd see that they were done in time.

And that's when I remembered what this dress was actually for.

God, what kind of daughter am I? I am terrible. I don't want this wedding to happen. My mother doesn't want this wedding to happen. So what am I doing, trying on a dress I'm supposed to be wearing at this event nobody but Grandmère wants to see happen, and which, if my dad succeeds, isn't going to happen anyway?

Still, I thought my heart might break as I took off the dress and put it back on its satin hanger. It was the most beautiful thing I had ever seen, let alone worn. If only, I couldn't help thinking, Michael could see me in this dress.

Or even Jo-C-rox. He might overcome his shyness and be able to tell me to my face what he'd been able to tell me before only in writing . . . and if it turns out he isn't that chili guy, maybe we could actually go out.

But there was only one appropriate place to wear a dress like this, and that was in a wedding. And no matter how much I wanted to wear that dress, I certainly didn't want there to be a wedding. My mother was barely holding on to her sanity as it was. A wedding at which John Tesh was in attendance—and who knows, maybe even singing—might push her over the edge.

Still, I've never in my life felt as much like a princess as I did in that dress.

Too bad I'll never get to wear it.

Wednesday, October 29, 10 p.m.

Okay, so I was just casually flipping through the channels, you know, taking a little study break and all from thinking up a profound moment to write about in my English journal, when all of a sudden I hit Channel 67, one of the public access channels, and there is an episode of Lilly's show, *Lilly Tells It Like It Is*, that I have never seen before. Which was weird, because *Lilly Tells It Like It Is* is usually on Friday nights.

Then I figured since this Friday is Halloween, maybe Lilly's show was being preempted for coverage of the parade in the Village or something.

So I'm sitting there, watching the show, and it turns out to be the slumber party episode. You know, the one we taped on Saturday, with all the other girls confessing their French-kissing exploits, and me dropping the eggplant out the window? Only Lilly had edited out any scene showing my face, so unless you knew Mia Thermopolis was the one in the pajamas with the strawberries all over them, you would never have known it was me.

All in all, pretty tame stuff. Maybe some really puritanical moms would get upset about the French-kissing, but there aren't too many of those in the five boroughs, which is the extent of the broadcast region.

Then the camera did this funny skittering thing, and when the picture got clear again, there was this close-up of my face. That's right. MY FACE. I was lying on the floor with this pillow under my head, talking in this sleepy way.

Then I remembered: At the slumber party, after everyone else had fallen asleep, Lilly and I had stayed awake, chatting.

And it turned out she'd been FILMING ME THE WHOLE TIME!

I was lying there going, "The thing I most want to do is start a place for stray and abandoned animals. Like I went to Rome once, and there were about eighty million cats there, roaming around the monuments. And they totally would have died if these nuns hadn't fed them and stuff. So the first thing I think I'll do is, I'll start a place where all the stray animals in Genovia will be taken care of. You know? And I'd never have any of them put to sleep, unless they were really sick or something. And there'll just be like all these dogs and cats, and maybe some dolphins and ocelots—"

Lilly's voice, disembodied, went, "Are there ocelots in Genovia?"

I went, "I hope so. Maybe not, though. But whatever. Any animals that need a home, they can come live there. And maybe I'll hire some Seeing Eye dog trainers, and they can come and train all the dogs to be Seeing Eye dogs. And then we can give them away free to blind people who need them. And then we can take the cats to hospitals and old people's homes, and let the patients pet them, because that always makes people feel better—except people like my grandmère, who hates cats. We can take dogs for them. Or maybe one of the ocelots."

Lilly's voice: "And that's going to be your first act when you become the ruler of Genovia?"

I said, sleepily, "Yeah, I think so. Maybe we could just

turn the whole castle into an animal shelter, you know? And like all the strays in Europe can come live there. Even those cats in Rome."

"Do you think your grandmère is going to like that? I mean, having all those stray cats around the castle?"

I said, "She'll be dead by then, so who cares?"

Oh, my God! I hope they don't have public access on the TVs up at the Plaza!

Lilly asked me, "What part of it do you hate the most? Being a princess, I mean."

"Oh, that's easy. Not being able to go to the deli to buy milk without having to call ahead and arrange for a bodyguard to escort me. Not being able just to come over and hang out with you without it being this big production. This whole thing with my fingernails. I mean, who cares how my fingernails look, right? Why does it even matter? That kind of stuff."

Lilly went, "Are you nervous? About your formal introduction to the people of Genovia, in December?"

"Well, not really nervous, just . . . I don't know. What if they don't like me? Like the ladies-in-waiting and stuff? I mean, nobody at school likes me. So chances are, nobody in Genovia will like me, either."

"People at school like you," Lilly said.

Then, right in front of the camera, I drifted off to sleep. Good thing I didn't drool, or worse, snore. I wouldn't have been able to show my face at school tomorrow.

Then these words floated up over the screen: *Don't Believe the Hype! This Is the* Real *Interview with the Princess of Genovia!*

As soon as it was over, I called Lilly and asked her exactly what she thought she'd been doing.

She just went, in this infuriatingly superior voice, "I just want people to be able to see the real Mia Thermopolis."

"No, you don't," I said. "You just want one of the networks to pick up on the interview, and pay you lots of money for it."

"Mia," Lilly said, sounding wounded. "How can you even think such a thing?"

She sounded so taken aback that I realized I must have been wrong about that one.

"Well," I said, "you could have told me."

"Would you have agreed to it?" Lilly wanted to know.

"Well," I said. "No . . . probably not."

"There you go," Lilly said.

I guess I don't come off as quite as much of a big-mouthed idiot in Lilly's interview. I just come off as a whacko who has a thing for cats. I really don't know which is worse.

But the truth is, I'm actually starting not to care. I wonder if this is what happens to celebrities. Like maybe at first, you really care what they say about you in the press, but after a while, you're just like, Whatever.

I do wonder if Michael saw this, and if so, what he thought of my pajamas. They are quite nice ones.

Hank didn't come to school with me today. He called first thing this morning and said he wasn't feeling too well. I am not surprised. Last night Mamaw and Papaw called wanting to know where in Manhattan they could go for a New York strip. Since I do not generally frequent restaurants that serve meat, I asked Mr. Gianini for a suggestion, and he made a reservation at this semi-famous steak place.

And then, in spite of my mother's strenuous objections, he insisted on taking Mamaw and Papaw and Hank and me out, so he could get to know his future in-laws better.

This was apparently too much for my mother. She actually got out of bed, put mascara and lipstick and a bra on, and went with us. I think it was mostly to guard against Mamaw driving Mr. G away with her many references to the number of family cars my mother accidentally rolled over in cornfields while she was learning to drive.

At the restaurant, I am horrified to report, in spite of the increased risk of heart disease and some cancers to which saturated fats and cholesterol have scientifically been linked, my future stepfather, my cousin, and my maternal grandparents—not to mention Lars, whom I had no idea was so fond of meat, and my mother, who attacked her steak like Rosemary attacked that raw chunk of ground round in *Rosemary's Baby* (which I've never actually seen, but I heard about it)—ingested what had to have been the equivalent of an entire cow.

This distressed me very much and I wanted to point out to them how unnecessary and unhealthy it is to eat things that were once alive and walking around, but, remembering my princess training, I merely concentrated on my entree of grilled vegetables and said nothing.

Still, I am not at all surprised Hank doesn't feel well. All that red meat is probably sitting, completely undigested, behind those washboard abs even as we speak. (I am only assuming Hank has washboard abs, since, thankfully, I have not actually seen them).

Interestingly, however, that was the one meal my mother has been able to keep down. This baby is no vegetarian, that's for sure.

Anyway, the disappointment Hank's absence has generated here at Albert Einstein is palpable. Miss Molina saw me in the hall and asked, sadly, "You don't need another guest pass for your cousin today?"

Hank's absence also apparently means that my special dispensation from the mean looks the cheerleaders have been giving me is revoked: This morning Lana reached out, snapped the back of my bra, and asked in her snottiest voice, "What are you wearing a bra for? You don't need one."

I long for a place where people treat each other with courtesy and respect. That, unfortunately, is not high school. Maybe in Genovia? Or possibly that space station the Russians built, the one that's falling apart above our heads.

Anyway, the only person who seems happy about Hank's misfortune is Boris Pelkowski. He was waiting for Lilly by the front doors to the school when we arrived this morning, and as soon as he saw us, he asked, "Where is Honk?"

(Because of his thick Russian accent, that's the way he pronounces Hank's name.)

"Honk—I mean, Hank—is sick," I informed him, and it would not be exaggerating to say that the look that spread across Boris's uneven features was beatific. It was actually a little bit touching. Boris's doglike devotion to Lilly can be annoying, but I know that I really only feel that way about it because I am envious. *I* want a boy I can tell all my deepest secrets to. *I* want a boy who will French-kiss me. *I* want a boy who will be jealous if I spend too much time with another guy, even a total bohunk like Hank.

But I guess we don't always get what we want, do we? It looks like all I'm going to get is a baby brother or sister, and a stepfather who knows a lot about the quadratic formula and who is moving in tomorrow with his foozball table.

Oh, and the rule of the throne of a country, someday.

Big deal. I'd rather have a boyfriend.

THINGS TO DO BEFORE MR. G MOVES IN

1. Vacuum
2. Clean out cat box
3. Drop off laundry
4. Take out recycling, esp. any of Mom's magazines that refer to orgasms on the cover—very imp.!!!
5. Remove feminine hygiene products from all bathrooms
6. Clear out space in living room for foozball table/ pinball machine/large TV
7. Check medicine cabinet: Hide Midol, Nair, Jolene—very imp.!!!
8. Remove *Our Bodies, Ourselves* and *The Joy of Sex* from Mom's bookshelves
9. Call cable company. Get Classic Sports Network added. Remove Romance Channel.
10. Get Mom to stop hanging bras on bedroom doorknob
11. Stop biting off fake fingernails
12. Stop thinking so much about M. M.
13. Fix lock on bathroom door
14. Toilet paper!!!!

I don't believe this.

They've done it again.

Hank and Lilly have disappeared AGAIN!

I didn't even know about the Hank part until Lars got a call on his cell phone from my mother. She was very annoyed, because her mother had called her at the studio, screaming hysterically because Hank was missing from his hotel room. Mom wanted to know if Hank had shown up at school.

Which, to the best of my knowledge, he had not.

Then Lilly didn't show up for lunch.

She wasn't even very subtle about it, either. We were doing the Presidential Fitness exam in PE, and just as it was her turn to climb the rope, Lilly started complaining that she had cramps.

Since Lilly complains that she has cramps every single time the Presidential Fitness exam rolls around, I wasn't suspicious. Mrs. Potts sent Lilly to the nurse's office, and I figured I'd see her at lunch, miraculously recovered.

But then she didn't show up for lunch. A consultation with the nurse revealed that Lilly's cramps had been of such severity, she'd decided to go home for the rest of the day.

Cramps. I am so sure. Lilly doesn't have cramps. What she has is the hots for my cousin!

The real question is, how long can we keep this from Boris? Remembering the Mahler we'd been subjected to yesterday, everyone is being careful not to remark how coincidental it is that Lilly is sick and Hank is missing in action at the same time. Nobody wants to have to resort to the gym mats again. Those things were heavy.

As a precaution, Michael is trying to keep Boris busy with a computer game he invented called Decapitate the Backstreet Boy. In it, you get to hurl knives and axes and stuff at members of the Backstreet Boys. The person who cuts the heads off the most Backstreet Boys moves up to another level, where he gets to cut off the heads of the boys in 98 Degrees, then 'N Sync, etc. The player who cuts off the most heads gets to carve his initials on Ricky Martin's naked chest.

I can't believe Michael only got a B on this game in his computer class. But the teacher took points off because he felt it wasn't violent enough for today's market.

Mrs. Hill is letting us talk today. I know it's because she doesn't want to have to listen to Boris play Mahler, or worse, Wagner. I went up to Mrs. Hill after class yesterday and apologized for what I said on TV about her always being in the teachers' lounge, even though it was the truth. She said not to worry about it. I'm pretty sure this is because my dad sent her a DVD player, along with a big bunch of flowers, the day after the interview was broadcast. She's been a lot nicer to me since then.

You know, I find all of this stuff about Lilly and Hank very difficult to process. I mean, *Lilly*, of all people, turning out to be such a slave to lust. Because she can't genuinely be in love with Hank. He's a nice enough guy and all—and very good-looking—but let's face it, his elevator does *not* go all the way up.

Lilly, on the other hand, belongs to Mensa—or at least

she could if she didn't think it hopelessly bourgeois. Plus Lilly isn't exactly what you'd call a traditional beauty—I mean, *I* think she's pretty, but according to today's admittedly limited ideal of what "attractive" is, Lilly doesn't really pass muster. She's much shorter than me, and kind of chunky, and has that sort of squished-in face. Not really the type you'd expect a guy like Hank to fall for.

So what do a girl like Lilly and a guy like Hank have in common, anyway?

Oh, God, don't answer that.

HOMEWORK

Algebra: pg. 123, problems 1–5, 7
English: in your journal, describe one day in your life; don't forget profound moment
World Civ: answer questions at end of Chapter 10
G&T: bring one dollar on Monday for earplugs
French: une description d'une personne, trente mots minimum
Biology: Kenny says not to worry, he'll do it for me

Another huge shock. If my life continues along this roller-coaster course, I may have to seek professional counseling.

When I walked in for my princess lesson, there was Mamaw—*Mamaw*—sitting on one of Grandmère's tiny pink couches, sipping tea.

"Oh, she was always like that," Mamaw was saying. "Stubborn as a mule."

I was sure they were talking about me. I threw down my bookbag and went, "I am *not!*"

Grandmère was sitting on the couch opposite Mamaw, a teacup and saucer poised in her hands. In the background, Vigo was running around like a little windup toy, answering the phone and saying things like, "No, the orange blossoms are for the wedding party, the roses are for the centerpieces," and "But *of course* the lamb chops were meant to be appetizers."

"What kind of way is that to enter a room?" Grandmère barked at me in French. "A princess never interrupts her elders, and she certainly never throws things. Now come here and greet me properly."

I went over and gave her a kiss on both cheeks, even though I didn't want to. Then I went over to Mamaw and did the same thing. Mamaw giggled and went, "How continental!"

Grandmère said, "Now sit down, and offer your grandmother a madeleine."

I sat down, to show how unstubborn I can be, and offered

Mamaw a madeleine from the plate on the table in front of her, the way Grandmère had shown me to.

Mamaw giggled again and took one of the cookies. She kept her pinky in the air as she did so.

"Why, thanks, hon," she said.

"Now," Grandmère said, in English. "Where were we, Shirley?"

Mamaw said, "Oh, yes. Well, as I was saying, she's always been that way. Just stubborn as the day is long. I'm not surprised she's dug her heels in about this wedding. Not surprised at all."

Hey, it wasn't me they were talking about after all. It was—

"I mean, I can't tell you we were thrilled when this happened the first time. 'Course, Helen never mentioned he was a prince. If we had known, we'd have encouraged her to marry him."

"Understandably," Grandmère murmured.

"But this time," Mamaw said, "well, we just couldn't be more thrilled. Frank is a real doll."

"Then we are agreed," Grandmère said. "This wedding must—and will—take place."

"Oh, definitely," Mamaw said.

I half expected them to spit in their hands and shake on it, an old Hoosier custom I learned from Hank.

But instead they each took a sip of their tea.

I was pretty sure nobody wanted to hear from me, but I cleared my throat anyway.

"Amelia," Grandmère said, in French. "Don't even think about it."

Too late. I said, "Mom doesn't want—"

"Vigo," Grandmère called. "Do you have those shoes? The ones that match the princess's dress?"

Like magic, Vigo appeared, carrying the prettiest pair of pink satin slippers I have ever seen. They had rosettes on the toes that matched the ones on my maid-of-honor dress.

"Aren't they lovely?" Vigo said, as he showed them to me. "Don't you want to try them on?"

It was cruel. It was underhanded.

It was Grandmère, all over.

But what could I do? I couldn't resist. The shoes fit perfectly, and looked, I have to admit, gorgeous on me. They gave my ski-like feet the appearance of being a size smaller—maybe even two sizes! I couldn't wait to wear them, and the dress, too. Maybe if the wedding was called off, I could wear them to the prom. If things worked out with Jo-C-rox, I mean.

"It would be a shame to have to send them back," Grandmère said with a sigh, "because your mother is being so stubborn."

Then again, maybe not.

"Couldn't I keep them for another occasion?" I asked. Hint, hint.

"Oh, no," Grandmère said. "Pink is so inappropriate for anything but a wedding."

Why me?

When my lesson was over—apparently today's consisted of sitting there listening to my two grandmothers complain about how their children (and grandchildren) don't appreciate them—Grandmère stood up and said to Mamaw, "So we understand each other, Shirley?"

And Mamaw said, "Oh, yes, Your Highness."

This sounded very ominous to me. In fact, the more I think about it, the more convinced I am that my dad hasn't done a single solitary thing to bail Mom out of what is clearly going to be a very messy situation. According to Grandmère, a limo is going to swing by our place tomorrow evening to pick up me, Mom, and Mr. Gianini, and whisk us off to the Plaza. It's going to be pretty obvious to everyone when my mom refuses to get into the car that there isn't going to be any wedding.

I think I am going to have to take matters into my own hands. I know Dad assured me that everything is under control, but we're talking Grandmère. GRANDMÈRE!

During the ride downtown I tried pumping Mamaw for information—you know, about what she and Grandmère meant when they said they "understood" one another.

But she wouldn't tell me a thing . . . except that she and Papaw were too tired, what with all the sightseeing they've been doing—not to mention worrying about Hank, whom they still hadn't heard from—to go out for dinner tonight, and were going to stay in and order room service.

Which is just as well, because I'm pretty sure if I have to hear one more person say the words "medium rare," I might hurl.

Well, Mr. Gianini is all moved in. I have already played nine games of foozball. Boy, are my wrists tired.

It's not really weird having him here on a permanent basis, because he was always hanging around before anyway. The only difference really is the big TV, the pinball machine, the foozball table, and the drum set in the corner where we normally keep Mom's life-size metallic gold bust of Elvis.

But the coolest thing is the pinball machine. It's called Motorcycle Gang, and it has all these very realistic drawings of tattooed, leather-wearing Hell's Angels on it. Also, it has pictures of the Hell's Angels' girlfriends—who don't have very much clothing on at all—bending over and sticking out their enormous bosoms. When you sink a ball, the pinball machine makes the noise of a motorcycle engine revving very loudly.

My mother took one look at it and just stood there, shaking her head.

I know it's misogynistic and sexist and all, but it's also really, really neat.

Mr. Gianini told me today that he thought it would be all right for me to call him Frank now, considering the fact that we are practically related. But I just can't bring myself to do it. So I just call him Hey. I go, "Hey, can you pass the parmesan?" and "Hey, have you seen the remote control?"

See? No names needed. Pretty clever, huh?

Of course, it hasn't exactly been smooth sailing. There's the small fact that tomorrow, there's supposedly going to be this huge celebrity wedding that I know has not been canceled, and that I also know my mother still hasn't the slightest intention of attending.

But when I ask her about it, instead of freaking out, my mom just smiles all secretively, and says, "Don't worry about it, Mia."

But how can I help worrying about it? The only thing that is definitely off is my mom and Mr. G's trip to the courthouse. I asked if they still wanted me to come dressed as the Empire State Building, thinking I should probably start working on my costume, and all, and my mom just got this furtive look in her eyes and said why don't we just hold off on that.

I could kind of tell she didn't want to talk about it, so I clammed up and went and called Lilly. I figured it was about time she gave me some explanation as to just what was going on here.

But when I called her, the line was busy. Which meant there was a good chance Lilly or Michael was online. I took a gamble and instant-messaged Lilly. She wrote back right away.

FtLouie: Lilly, just where did you and Hank disappear to today? And don't lie and say you weren't together.
WmnRule: I fail to see what business it is of yours.
FtLouie: Well, let's just say that if you want to hang on to your boyfriend, you better come up with a good explanation.
WmnRule: I have a very good explanation. But I am not likely to share it with you. You'll just blab it to Beverly Bellerieve. Oh, and twenty-two million viewers.

FTLOUIE: That is so totally unfair. Look, Lilly, I'm worried about you. It isn't like you to skip school. What about your book about high school society? You may have missed out on some valuable material for it.

WMNRULE: Oh, really? Did something happen today worth recording?

FTLOUIE: Well, some of the seniors snuck into the teachers' lounge and put a fetal pig in the mini-fridge.

WMNRULE: Gosh, I'm so sorry I missed that. Is there anything else, Mia? Because I am trying to research something on the Web right now.

Yes, there was something else. Didn't she know how wrong it was to be seeing two boys at the same time? Especially when some of us don't even have *one* boy? Couldn't she see how selfish and mean-spirited that was?

But I didn't write that. Instead, I wrote:

FTLOUIE: Well, Boris was pretty upset, Lilly. I mean, he totally suspects something.

WMNRULE: Boris has got to learn that in a loving relationship, it is important to establish bonds of trust. That is something you might keep in mind yourself, Mia.

I realize, of course, that Lilly is talking about *our* relationship—hers and mine. But if you think about it, it applies to more than just Lilly and Boris, and Lilly and me. It applies to me and my dad, too. And me and my mom. And me and . . . well, just about everybody.

Was this, I wondered, a profound moment? Should I get

out my English journal?

It was right after this that it happened: I got instant-messaged by someone else. By Jo-C-rox himself!

JoCROX: So are you going to *Rocky Horror* tomorrow?

Oh, my God. Oh, my GOD. OH, MY GOD!

Jo-C-rox is going to *Rocky Horror* tomorrow.

And so is Michael.

Really, there is only one logical explanation that can be drawn from this: Jo-C-rox is Michael. Michael is Jo-C-rox. He HAS to be. He just HAS to be.

Right?

I didn't know what to do. I wanted to jump up from my computer and run around my room and scream and laugh at the same time.

Instead—and I don't know where I got the presence of mind to do this, I wrote back:

FTLOUIE: I hope so.

I can't believe it. I really can't believe it. Michael is Jo-C-rox.

Right?

What am I going to do? What am I going to do?

Friday, October 31, Homeroom

I woke with the strangest feeling of foreboding. I couldn't figure out why for a few minutes. I lay there in bed, listening to the rain patter against my window. Fat Louie was at the end of my bed, kneading the comforter and purring very loudly.

Then I remembered: Today, according to my grandmother, is the day my pregnant mother is supposed to marry my Algebra teacher in a huge ceremony at the Plaza Hotel, with musical accompaniment courtesy of John Tesh.

I lay there for a minute, wishing my temperature was one hundred and two again, so I wouldn't have to get out of bed and face what was sure to be a day of drama and hurt feelings.

And then I remembered my e-mail from the night before, and jumped right out of bed.

Michael is my secret admirer! Michael is Jo-C-rox!

And with any luck, by the end of the night, he'll have admitted it to my face!

Mr. Gianini is not here today. Instead, we have a substitute teacher named Mrs. Krakowski.

It is very strange that Mr. G isn't here, because he was certainly in the loft this morning. We played a game of foozball before Lars showed up in the limo. We even offered Mr. G a ride to school, but he said he was coming in later.

Really later, it looks like.

A lot of people aren't here today, actually. Michael, for instance, didn't catch a ride with us this morning. Lilly says that is because he had last-minute problems printing out a paper that is due today.

But I wonder if it is really because he is too scared to face me after admitting that he is Jo-C-rox.

Well, not that he actually admitted it. But he sort of did. Didn't he?

Mr. Howell is three times as old as Gilligan. The difference in their ages is 48. How old are Mr. Howell and Gilligan?

$T =$ Gilligan
$3T =$ Mr. Howell

$3T - T = 48$
$2T = 48$
$T = 24$

Oh, Mr G, where ARE you?

Okay.

I will never underestimate Lilly Moscovitz again. Nor will I suspect her of having anything but the most altruistic motives. This I hereby solemnly swear in writing.

It was at lunch when it happened:

We were all sitting there—me, my bodyguard, Tina Hakim Baba and her bodyguard, Lilly, Boris, Shameeka, and Ling Su. Michael, of course, sits over with the rest of the Computer Club, so he wasn't there, but everybody else who mattered was.

Shameeka was reading aloud to us from some of the brochures her father had gotten from girls' schools in New Hampshire. Each one filled Shameeka with more terror, and me with more shame for ever having opened my big mouth in the first place.

Suddenly, a shadow fell over our little table.

We looked up.

There stood an apparition of such godlike stature that for a minute, I think even Lilly believed the chosen people's long lost Messiah had finally shown up.

It turned out it was only Hank—but Hank looking as I had certainly never seen him before. He had on a black cashmere sweater beneath a clinging black leather coat, and black jeans that seemed to go on and on over his long, lean legs. His golden hair had been expertly styled and cut, and—I swear—he looked so much like Keanu Reeves in *The Matrix* that I actually might have believed he had wandered in off the set if it hadn't been for the fact that on his feet, he wore cowboy boots. Black, expensive-looking ones, but cowboy boots, just the same.

I don't think it was my imagination that the entire crowd inside the cafeteria seemed to gasp as Hank slid into a chair at our table—the reject table, I have frequently heard it called.

"Hello, Mia," Hank said.

I stared at him. It wasn't just the clothes. There was something . . . different about him. His voice seemed deeper, somehow. And he smelled . . . well, good.

"So," Lilly said to him, as she scooped a glob of creamy filling out of her Ring Ding. "How'd it go?"

"Well," Hank said, in that same deep voice. "You're looking at Calvin Klein's newest underwear model."

Lilly sucked the filling off her finger. "Hmmm," she said, with her mouth full. "Good for you."

"I owe it all to you, Lilly," Hank said. "If it weren't for you, they never would have signed me."

Then it hit me. The reason Hank seemed so different was that his Hoosier drawl was gone!

"Now, Hank," Lilly said. "We discussed this. It's your natural ability that got you where you are. I just gave you a few pointers."

When Hank turned his gaze toward me, I saw that his sky-blue eyes were damp. "Your friend Lilly," he said, "has done something no one's ever done for me in my life."

I threw an accusing gaze at Lilly.

I knew it. I *knew* they'd had sex.

But then Hank said, "She believed in me, Mia. Believed in me enough to help me pursue my dream . . . a dream I've had since I was a very young boy. A lot of people—including my own Mamaw and Pa—I mean, my grandparents—told me it was a pipe dream. They told me to give it up, that it would never happen. But when I told my dream to Lilly, she held out her hand"—Hank held out his hand to illustrate this, and all of us—me, Lars, Tina, Tina's bodyguard Wahim, Shameeka, and Ling Su—looked at that hand, the nails of which had been perfectly manicured—"and said, 'Come with me, Hank. I will help you achieve your dream.'"

Hank put his hand down. "And do you know what?"

All of us—except Lilly, who went right on eating—were so astonished, we could only stare.

Hank did not wait for us to reply. He said, "It happened. Today, it happened. My dream came true. I was signed by Ford. I am their newest male model."

We all blinked at him.

"And I owe it all," Hank said, "to this woman here."

Then something really shocking happened. Hank got up out of his chair, walked over to where Lilly was sitting, innocently finishing her Ring Ding, not suspecting a thing, and pulled her to a standing position.

Then as everyone in the entire cafeteria looked on—including, I noticed, Lana Weinberger and all her cronies over at the cheerleaders' table—my cousin Hank laid such a kiss on Lilly Moscovitz, I thought he just might suck that Ring Ding right back up again.

When he was done kissing her, Hank let go. And Lilly, looking as if someone had just poked her with an electric prod, sank slowly back down to her seat. Hank adjusted the lapels of his leather coat and turned to me.

"Mia," he said. "Tell Mamaw and Papaw they're going to have to find somebody to cover my shift at the hardware store. I ain't—I mean, I'm *not*—going back to Versailles. Ever."

And with that, he strode from our cafeteria like a cowboy walking away from a gunfight he'd just won.

Or I suppose I should say he *started* to stride from the cafeteria. Unfortunately for Hank, he didn't make it out quite fast enough.

Because one of the people who had observed that searing kiss he'd laid on Lilly was none other than Boris Pelkowski.

And it was Boris Pelkowski—Boris Pelkowski, with his retainer and his sweater tucked into his pants—who stood up and said, "Not so fast, hot shot."

I'm not sure if Boris had just seen the movie *Top Gun* or what, but that *hot shot* came out sounding pretty menacing, considering Boris's accent and all.

Hank kept going. I don't know if he hadn't heard Boris, or if he wasn't about to let some little violin-playing genius mess up his great exit.

Then Boris did something completely reckless. He reached out and grabbed Hank by the arm as he went by and said, "That's *my* girl you had your lips all over, pretty boy."

I am not even joking. Those were his exact words. Oh, how my heart thrilled to hear them! If only some guy (okay, Michael) would say something like that about me. Not the Josiest girl he'd ever met, but *his* girl. Boris had actually referred to Lilly as *his* girl! No boy has ever referred to me as *his* girl. Oh, I know all about feminism and how women aren't property and it's sexist to go around claiming them as such. But, oh! If only somebody (okay, Michael) would say I was *his* girl!

Anyway, Hank just went, "Huh?"

And then, from out of nowhere, Boris's fist went sailing into Hank's face. *Pow!*

Only it didn't really sound like pow. It sounded more like a thud. There was a sickening crunch of bones splintering. All of us girls gasped, thinking that Boris had marred Hank's perfect cover-guy face.

But we needn't have worried: It was Boris's hand that made the crunching sound, not Hank's face. Hank escaped completely unscathed. Boris is the one who has to have his knuckles splinted.

And you know what that means:

No more Mahler.

Whoopee!!!

It's unprincess-like of me, however, to gloat over another's misfortune.

I borrowed Lars's cell phone and called the SoHo Grand between lunch and fifth period. I mean, I figured someone should let Mamaw and Papaw know that Hank was all right. Well, a Ford model, but all right.

Mamaw must have been sitting by the phone, since she picked up on the first ring.

"Clarisse?" she said. "I still haven't heard from them."

Which is weird. Because Clarisse is Grandmère's name.

"Mamaw?" I said. "It's me, Mia."

"Oh, *Mia*." Mamaw laughed a little. "I'm sorry, honey. I thought you were the princess. I mean, the dowager princess. Your other grandma."

I went, "Uh, yeah. Well, it's not. It's me. And I'm just calling to tell you that I heard from Hank."

Mamaw shrieked so loud, I had to hold the cell phone away from my ear.

"WHERE IS HE?" she yelled. "YOU TELL HIM FROM ME THAT WHEN I GET MY HANDS ON HIM, HE'S—"

"Mamaw," I cried. It was kind of embarrassing, because all sorts of people in the hallway heard her yelling and were looking at me. I tried to make myself inconspicuous by hunching behind Lars.

"Mamaw," I said, "he got a contract with Ford Models, Inc. He's the newest Calvin Klein underwear model. He's going to be a big celebrity, like—"

"UNDERWEAR?" Mamaw yelled. "Mia, you tell that boy to call me RIGHT NOW."

"Well, I can't really do that, Mamaw," I said. "On account of the fact that—"

"RIGHT NOW," Mamaw repeated, "or he's in BIG TROUBLE."

"Um," I said. The bell was ringing anyway. "Okay, Mamaw. Is, um, the, uh, wedding still on?"

"The WHAT?"

"The wedding," I said, wishing I could, just for once, be a normal girl who did not have to go around asking people if the royal marriage of her pregnant mother and her Algebra teacher was still on.

"Well, of course it's still on," Mamaw said. "What do you think?"

"Oh," I said. "You, um, talked to my mom?"

"Of course I did," Mamaw said. "Everything is all set."

"Really?" I was immensely surprised. I could not picture my mother going along with this thing. Not in a million years. "And she said she'd be there?"

"Well, of course she'll be there," Mamaw said. "It's her wedding, isn't it?"

Well . . . sort of, I guess. I didn't say that to Mamaw, though. I said, "Sure." And then I hung up, feeling crushed.

For entirely selfish reasons, too, I confess. I was a little bit sad for my mom, I guess, since she really had tried to put up a resistance against Grandmère. I mean, she really had tried. It wasn't her fault, of course, that she'd been going up against such a inexorable force.

But mostly I felt sad for myself. I would NEVER escape in time for *Rocky Horror*. Never, never, *never*. I mean, I know the movie doesn't even start until midnight, but wedding receptions last way longer than that.

And who knows if Michael will ever ask me out again? I mean, not once today has he acknowledged that he is, in fact, Jo-C-rox, nor has he mentioned *Rocky Horror*. Not once. Not even so much as a reference to Rachel Leigh Cook.

And we talked at length during G and T. AT LENGTH. That is on account of how some of us who saw last year's groundbreaking episode of *Lilly Tells It Like It Is* were understandably confused by Lilly's helping Hank to realize his dream of supermodel stardom. The segment was titled "Yes, You as an Individual *Can* Bring Down the Sexist, Racist, Ageist, and Sizeist Modeling Industry" (by "criticizing ads that demean women and limit our ideas of beauty" and "finding ways to make your protest known to the companies advertised" and "letting the media know you want to see more varied and realistic images of women." Also, Lilly urged us to "challenge men who judge, choose, and discard women on the basis of appearance").

The following exchange took place during Gifted and Talented (Mrs. Hill has returned to the teachers' lounge—permanently, one can only hope) and included Michael Moscovitz, who, as you will see, did NOT ONCE mention Jo-C-rox or *Rocky Horror*:

Me: Lilly, I thought you found the modeling industry as a whole sexist and racist and belittling to the human race.

Lilly: So? What's your point?

Me: Well, according to Hank, you helped him realize his

dream of becoming a you know what. A model.

Lilly: Mia, when I recognize a human soul crying out for self-actualization, I am powerless to stop myself. I must do what I can to see that that person's dream is realized.

[Gee, I haven't noticed Lilly doing all that much to help me realize *my* dream of French-kissing her brother. But on the other hand, I have not exactly made that dream known to her.]

Me: Um, Lilly, I hadn't noticed that you had a real foothold in the modeling industry.

Lilly: I don't. I merely taught your cousin how to make the most of his God-given talents. Some simple lessons in elocution and fashion, and he was well on his way to landing that contract with Ford.

Me: Well, why did it have to be such a big secret?

Lilly: Do you have any idea how fragile the male ego is?

[Here Michael broke in.]

Michael: Hey!

Lilly: I'm sorry, but it's true. Hank's self-esteem had already been reduced to nothing thanks to Amber, Corn Queen of Versailles County. I couldn't allow any negative comments to ruin what little self-confidence he had left. You know how fatalistic boys can be.

Michael: Hey!

Lilly: It was vital that Hank be allowed to pursue his dream without the slightest fatalistic influence. Otherwise, I knew, he didn't stand a chance. And so I kept our plan a secret even from those I most cared about. Any one of you, without consciously meaning to, might have torpedoed Hank's chances with the most casual of comments.

Me: Come on. We'd have been supportive.

Lilly: Mia, think about it. If Hank had said to you, 'Mia, I want to be a model,' what would you have done? Come on. You would have laughed.

Me: No, I wouldn't have.

Lilly: Yes, you would have. Because to you, Hank is your whiny, allergy-prone cousin from the boondocks who doesn't even know what a bagel is. But I, you see, was able to look beyond that, to the man Hank had the potential to become. . . .

Michael: Yeah, a man who is destined to have his own pin-up calendar.

Lilly: You, Michael, are just jealous.

Michael: Oh, yeah. I've always wanted a big picture of myself in my underwear hanging up in Times Square.

[Actually, I think that is something I would really enjoy seeing, but Michael was, of course, being sarcastic.]

Michael: You know, Lil, I highly doubt Mom and Dad are going to be so impressed by your tremendous act of charity that they're going to overlook the fact that you skipped school to do it. Especially when they find out you've got detention next week because of it.

Lilly: (looking long-suffering) The most eleemosynary are often martyred.

And that was it. That's all he said to me, all day. ALL DAY.

Note to self: look up *eleemosynary*

POSSIBLE REASONS MICHAEL WON'T ADMIT HE IS JO-C-ROX

1. He really is too shy to reveal his true feelings for me.
2. He thinks I don't feel the same way about him.
3. He's changed his mind and doesn't like me after all.
4. He doesn't want to have to bear the social stigma of dating a freshman and he is just waiting until I am a sophomore before asking me out. (Except that by then he'll be a freshman in college and won't want to bear the social stigma of dating a high school girl.)
5. He isn't Jo-C-rox at all and it turns out I am obsessing about something written by that guy from the cafeteria who has the thing about corn.

HOMEWORK

Algebra: none (no Mr. G!)
English: finish Day in a Life! Plus Profound Moment!
World Civ: read and analyze one current event from Sunday Times (200 wd minimum)
G&T: don't forget the dollar!
French: pg. 120, huit phrases (ex. A)
Biology: questions at end of Chapter 12—get answers from Kenny!

ENGLISH JOURNAL

A Day In My Life by Mia Thermopolis
(I chose to write about a night instead.
Is that okay, Mrs. Spears?)

FRIDAY, OCTOBER 31

3:16 p.m.—Arrive home at SoHo loft with bodyguard (Lars). Find it ostensibly empty. Decide mother probably napping (something she does a lot these days).

3:18 p.m.–3:45 p.m.—Play foozball with bodyguard. Win three out of twelve games. Decide must practice foozball in spare time.

3:50 p.m.—Curious as to why riotous game of foozball—not to mention incredibly loud pinball machine—have not awakened mother from nap. Knock gently on bedroom door. Stand there hoping door does not open and reveal view of mother actually sharing bed with Algebra teacher.

3:51 p.m.—Knock louder. Decide perhaps cannot be heard due to intense lovemaking session. Sincerely hope I will not be inadvertent witness to any nakedness.

3:52 p.m.—After receiving no response to my knock, I go into mother's bedroom. No one is there! Check of mother's bathroom reveals crucial items such as mascara, lipstick, and bottle of folic acid tablets missing from medicine cabinet. Begin to suspect something is afoot.

3:55 p.m.—Phone rings. I answer it. It is my father.

Following conversation ensues:

Me: Dad? Mom's missing. And so is Mr. Gianini. He didn't even come to school today.

Father: You still call him Mr. Gianini even though he lives with you?

Me: Dad. Where are they?

Father: Don't worry about it.

Me: That woman is carrying my last chance at having a sibling. How can I help but worry about her?

Father: Everything is under control.

Me: How am I supposed to believe that?

Father: Because I said so.

Me: Dad, I think you should know, I have some very serious trust issues concerning you.

Father: How come?

Me: Well, part of it might be the fact that up until about a month ago, you had lied to me for my entire life about who you are and what you do for a living.

Father: Oh.

Me: So just tell me. WHERE IS MY MOTHER?

Father: She left you a letter. You can have it at eight o'clock.

Me: Dad, eight o'clock is when the wedding is supposed to start.

Father: I am aware of that.

Me: Dad, you can't do this to me. What am I supposed to tell—

Voice: Phillipe, is everything all right?

Me: Who is that? Who *is* that, Dad? Is that Beverly Bellerieve?

Father: I have to go now, Mia.
Me: No, Dad, wait—
CLICK

4:00 p.m.–4:15 p.m.–Tear apartment apart, looking for clues as to where mother might have disappeared to. Find none.

4:20 p.m.–Phone rings. Paternal grandmother on line. Requests to know if mother and I are ready for trip to salon for beauty makeover. Inform her that mother has left already (well, it's the truth, isn't it?). Grandmother suspicious. Inform her that if she has any questions to consult with her son, my father. Grandmother says she fully intends to do so. Also says limo will be by at five o'clock to pick me up.

5:00 p.m.–Limo pulls up. Bodyguard and I get into it. Inside is paternal grandmother (hereafter known as Grandmère) and maternal grandmother (hereafter known as Mamaw). Mamaw is very excited about upcoming nuptials–though excitement is somewhat dampened by cousin's desertion to become male supermodel. Grandmère, on other hand, is mysteriously calm. Says son (my father) has informed her that bride has decided to make own hair and make-up plans. Remembering missing folic acid tablets, I say nothing.

5:20 p.m.–Enter Chez Paolo.

6:45 p.m.–Emerge from Chez Paolo. Amazed at difference Paolo has made with Mamaw's hair. She no longer resembles mom in John Hughes film, but member of upscale country club.

7:00 p.m.—Arrive at Plaza. Father attributes bride's absence to her desire to nap before ceremony. When I surreptitiously force Lars to call home on his cell phone, however, no one answers.

7:15 p.m.—Begins to rain again. Mamaw observes that rain on a wedding day is bad luck. Grandmère says, No, that's pearls. Mamaw says, No, rain. First sign of division within formerly united ranks of grandmas.

7:30 p.m.—I am ushered into little chamber just off the White and Gold Room, where I sit with the other bridesmaids (supermodels Gisele, Karmen Kass, and Amber Valetta, whom Grandmère has hired due to fact that my mother refused to supply her with list of her own bridesmaids). I have changed into my beautiful pink dress and matching shoes.

7:40 p.m.—None of the other bridesmaids will talk to me, except to comment about how I look so "sweet." All they can talk about is a party they went to last night where someone threw up on Claudia Schiffer's shoes.

7:45 p.m.—Guests begin to arrive. I fail to recognize my maternal grandfather without his baseball cap. He looks quite spry in his tux. A little like an elderly Matt Damon.

7:47 p.m.—Two people arrive who claim to be parents of the groom. Mr. Gianini's parents from Long Island! Mr. Gianini Sr. calls Vigo "Bucko." Vigo looks delighted.

7:48 p.m.—Martha Stewart stands near door, chatting with Donald Trump about Manhattan real estate. She can't find a building with a co-op board that will let her keep her pet chinchillas.

7:50 p.m.—John Tesh has cut his hair. Almost don't recognize him. Looks faintly babe-like. Queen of Sweden asks him if he is friend of bride or groom. Says groom, for some inexplicable reason, though I happen to know from having looked through Mr. Gianini's CDs that he owns nothing but the Rolling Stones and a little Who.

7:55 p.m.—Everyone goes quiet as John Tesh sits down at baby grand. Pray that my mother is in different hemisphere and cannot see or hear this.

8:00 p.m.—Everyone waits expectantly. I demand that my father, who has joined me and the supermodels, give me letter from my mother. Dad surrenders letter.

8:01 p.m.—I read letter.

8:02 p.m.—I have to sit down.

8:05 p.m.—Grandmère and Vigo in deep consultation. They seem to have realized that neither the bride nor the groom have shown up.

8:07 p.m.—Amber Valetta whispers that if we don't get a move on, she's going to be late for a dinner engagement with Hugh Grant.

8:10 p.m.—A hush falls over the guests as my father, looking excessively princely in his tux (in spite of his bald head) strides to the front of the White and Gold Room. John Tesh stops playing.

8:11 p.m.—My father makes the following announcement:

Father: I want to thank all of you for taking the time out of your busy schedules to come here tonight. Unfortunately, the wedding between Helen Thermopolis and Frank Gianini will not take place . . . at least, not this evening. The happy couple have given us the slip, and this morning they flew to Cancun, where I understand they plan to be married by a justice of the peace.

[A shriek is heard from the far side of the baby grand. It does not appear to have come from John Tesh, but rather, Grandmère.]

Father: You are of course urged to join us in the Grand Ballroom for dinner. And thank you again for coming.

[Father strides off. Bewildered guests gather their belongings and go in search of cocktails. No sound whatsoever is heard from behind baby grand.]

Me: (to no one in particular) Mexico! They must be crazy. If my mother drinks the water, my future brother or sister will be born with flippers for feet!

Amber: Don't worry, my friend Heather got pregnant in Mexico, and she drank the water, and she just gave birth to twins.

Me: And they had dorsal fins coming out of their backs, didn't they?

8:20 p.m.–John Tesh begins to play. At least until Grandmère barks, "Oh, shut up!"

What the letter from my mother said:

Dear Mia,

By the time you read this, Frank and I will be married. I am sorry I couldn't tell you sooner, but when your grandmother asks you if you knew (and she will ask you), I wanted to be sure you could say truthfully that you didn't, so there won't be any ill feeling between the two of you.

[Ill feeling between Grandmère and me? Who does she think she's kidding? There's nothing but ill feeling between us!

Well, as far I'm concerned, anyway.]

More than anything, Frank and I wanted you to be there for our wedding. So we have decided that when we get back, we're going to have another ceremony: This one will be kept strictly secret and very private, with just our little family and our friends!

[Well, that certainly should be interesting. Most of my mom's friends are militant feminists or performance artists. One of them likes to stand up on a stage and pour chocolate syrup all over her naked body while reciting poetry.

I wonder how they are going to get along with Mr. G's friends, who I understand like to watch a lot of sports.]

You have been a tower of strength during this crazy time, Mia, and I want you to know how much I—as well as your father, and stepfather—appreciate it. You are the best daughter a mother could have, and this new little guy (or girl) is the luckiest baby in the world to have you as a big sister.

Missing you already—
Mom

I am in shock. I really am.

Not because my mom and my Algebra teacher eloped. That's kind of romantic, if you ask me.

No, it's the fact that my dad—*my dad*—helped them to do it. He actually defied his mother. In a BIG way.

In fact, because of all this, I'm starting to think my dad isn't scared of Grandmère at all! I think he just doesn't want to be bothered. I think he just feels it's easier to go along with her than to fight her, because fighting her is so messy and exhausting.

But not this time. This time, he put his foot down.

And you can bet he's going to pay for it, too.

I may never get over this. I am going to have to readjust everything I ever thought about him. Kind of like when Luke Skywalker finds out his dad is really Darth Vader. Only the opposite.

Anyway, while Grandmère was plotzing behind the baby grand, I went up to Dad and threw my arms around him and was like, "You did it!"

He looked at me curiously. "Why do you sound surprised?"

Oops. I said, totally embarrassed, "Oh, well, because, you know."

"No, I don't know."

"Well," I said. (WHY? WHY do I have such a big mouth?)

I thought about lying. But I think my dad must have realized what I was thinking, since he said, in this warning voice, "*Mia . . .*"

"Oh, okay," I said, grudgingly, letting him go. "It's just that sometimes you give the appearance—just the appearance, mind you—of being a little bit scared of Grandmère."

My dad reached out and wrapped an arm around my neck. He did this right in front of Liz Smith, who was getting up to follow everyone into the Grand Ballroom. She smiled at us as if she thought it was sweet, though.

"Mia," my dad said. "I am not scared of my mother. She really isn't as bad as you think. She just needs proper handling."

This was news to me.

"Besides," my dad said, "do you really think I would ever let you down? Or your mother? I will always be there for you two."

This was so nice, I actually got tears in my eyes for a minute. But it might have been the smoke from all the cigarettes. There were a lot of French people at this party.

"Mia, I haven't done so badly by you, have I?" my dad asked, all of a sudden.

I was surprised by the question. "No, Dad, of course not. You guys have always been okay parents."

My dad nodded. "I see."

I could see I hadn't been complimentary enough, so I added, "No, I mean it. I really couldn't ask for better . . ." I couldn't help adding, "I could probably live without the princess thing, though."

He looked as if he probably would have reached out and

ruffled my hair if it hadn't been so full of mousse his hand would have stuck to it.

"Sorry about that," he said. "But do you really think you'd be happy, Mia, being Nancy Normal Teenager?"

Um. Yes.

Except I wouldn't want my name to be Nancy.

We might have gone on to have a really profound moment I could have written about in my English journal if Vigo hadn't come hurrying up just then. He looked frazzled. And why not? His wedding was turning out to be a disaster! First the bride and groom had neglected to show up, and now the hostess, the dowager princess, had locked herself into her hotel suite and would not come out.

"What do you mean, she won't come out?" my father demanded.

"Just what I said, Your Highness." Vigo looked like he was about to start crying. "I have never seen her so angry! She says she has been betrayed by her own family, and she will never be able to show her face in public again, the shame is so great."

My dad looked heavenward. "Let's go," he said.

When we got to the door to the penthouse suite, my dad signaled for Vigo and me to be quiet. Then he knocked on the door.

"Mother," he called. "Mother, it's Phillipe. May I come in?"

No response. But I could tell she was in there. I could hear Rommel moaning softly.

"Mother," my dad said. He tried turning the door

handle, and found it locked. This caused him to sigh very deeply.

Well, you could see why. He had already spent the better part of the day thwarting all of her well-laid plans. That had to have been exhausting. And now *this*?

"Mother," he said. "I want you to open this door."

Still no response.

"Mother," my father said. "You are being ridiculous. I want you to open this door this instant. If you don't do it, I shall fetch the housekeeper, and have her open it for me. Are you trying to force me to resort to this? Is that it?"

I knew Grandmère would sooner let us see her without her makeup than ever allow a member of the hotel staff to be privy to one of our family squabbles, so I laid a hand on my dad's arm and whispered, "Dad, let me try."

My father shrugged, and, with a sort of if-you-want-to look, stepped aside.

I called through the door, "Grandmère? Grandmère, it's me, Mia."

I don't know what I'd expected. Certainly not for her to open the door. I mean, if she wouldn't do it for Vigo, whom she seemed to adore, or for her own son, who, if she didn't adore, was at least her only child, why would she do it for me?

But I was greeted with only silence from behind that door. Well, except for Rommel's whining.

I refused to be daunted, however. I raised my voice and called, "I'm really sorry about my mom and Mr. Gianini, Grandmère. But you have to admit it, I warned you that she didn't want this wedding. Remember? I told you she wanted something small. You might have realized that by the fact that there isn't a single person here who was actually invited by my mother. These are all *your* friends. Well, except for Mamaw and Papaw. And Mr. G's parents. But I mean, come on. My mom does not know Imelda Marcos, okay? And Barbara Bush? I'm sure she's a very nice lady, but not one of my mom's closest buddies."

Still no response.

"Grandmère," I called through the door. "Look, I am really surprised at you. I thought you were always teaching me that a princess has to be strong. I thought you said that a princess, no matter what kind of adversity she is facing, has to put on a brave face and not hide behind her wealth and privilege. Well, isn't that exactly what you're doing right now? Shouldn't you be down there right now, pretending this was exactly the way you planned things to go, and raising a glass to the happy couple in absentia?"

I jumped back as the doorknob to my grandmother's suite slowly turned. A second later, Grandmère came out, a vision in purple velvet and a diamond tiara.

She said, with a great deal of dignity, "I had every intention of returning to the party. I merely came up here to freshen my lipstick."

My dad and I exchanged glances.

"Sure, Grandmère," I said. "Whatever you say."

"A princess," Grandmère said, closing the door to her suite behind her, "never leaves her guests unattended."

"Okay," I said.

"So what are you two doing here?" Grandmère glared at my dad and me.

"We were, um, just checking on you," I explained.

"I see." Then Grandmère did a surprising thing. She slipped her hand through the crook of my elbow. Then, without looking at my dad, she said, "Come along."

I saw my dad roll his eyes at this blatant dis.

But he didn't look scared, the way *I* would have been.

"Hold on, Grandmère," I said.

Then I slipped my hand through the crook of my dad's elbow, so the three of us were standing in the hallway, linked by . . . well, by me.

Grandmère just sniffed and didn't say anything. But my dad smiled.

And you know what? I'm not sure, but I think it might have been a profound moment for all of us.

Well, all right. At least for *me*, anyway.

The evening wasn't a total bust.

Quite a few people seemed to have a very good time. Hank, for one. He actually showed up just in time for dinner—he'd always been good at that—looking totally gorgeous in an Armani tux.

Mamaw and Papaw were delighted to see him. Mrs. Gianini, Mr. Gianini's mom, took quite a shine to him, too. It must have been his clean-cut good manners. He hadn't forgotten any of Lilly's elocution lessons, and only mentioned his affection for 'muddin' on the weekends once. And later, when the dancing started, he asked Grandmère for the second waltz—Dad got the first—forever cementing him in her mind as the ideal royal consort for me.

Thank God first-cousin marriages were made illegal in Genovia in 1907.

But the happiest people I talked to all evening weren't actually at the party. No, at around ten o'clock, Lars handed me his cell phone, and when I said, "Hello?" wondering who it could be, my mom's voice, sounding very far away and crackly, went, "Mia?"

I didn't want to say the word 'Mom' too loudly, since I knew Grandmère was hovering nearby. And I don't think it likely that Grandmère is going to forgive my parents anytime soon for the fast one they pulled. I ducked behind a pillar and whispered, "Hey, Mom! Mr. Gianini make an honest woman out of you yet?"

Well, he had. The deed was done (a little late, if you ask me, but hey, at least the kid won't be born harboring the stigma of illegitimacy like I've had to all my life). It was only like six o'clock where they were, and they were on a beach somewhere sipping (virgin) piña coladas. I made my mom promise not to have any more, because you can't trust the ice at those places.

"Parasites can exist in ice, Mom," I informed her. "There are these worms that live in the glaciers in Antarctica, you know. We studied them in Bio. They've been around for thousands of years. So even if the water's frozen, you can still get sick from it. You definitely only want to get ice made from bottled water. Here, why don't you put Mr. Gianini on the phone, and I'll tell him exactly what he has to do—"

My mom interrupted me.

"Mia," she said. "How are—" She cleared her throat. "How's my mother taking it?"

"Mamaw?" I looked in Mamaw's direction. The truth was, Mamaw was having the time of her life. She was thoroughly enjoying her gig as mother of the bride. So far, she'd gotten to dance with Prince Albert, who was there representing the royal family of Monaco, and Prince Andrew, who didn't seem to be missing Fergie one bit, if you asked me.

"Um," I said. "Mamaw's . . . really mad at you."

It was a lie, of course, but it was a lie I knew would make my mother happy. One of her favorite things to do is make her parents mad.

"Really, Mia?" she asked, breathlessly.

"Uh-huh," I said, watching as Papaw twirled Mamaw around practically into the champagne fountain. "They'll probably never speak to you again."

"Oh," Mom said happily. "Isn't that too bad?"

Sometimes my natural ability to lie actually comes in handy.

But unfortunately, right then our connection broke up. Well, at least Mom had heard my warning about the ice worms before we lost contact.

As for me, well, I can't say I had the time of my life—I mean, the only person even close to my age was Hank, and he was way too busy dancing with Gisele to talk to me.

Thankfully, around eleven, my dad was like, "Uh, Mia, isn't it Halloween?"

I said, "Yeah, Dad."

"Don't you have someplace you'd rather be?"

You know, I hadn't forgotten the whole *Rocky Horror* thing, but I figured Grandmère needed me. Sometimes family things are more important than friend things—even romance things.

But as soon as I heard that, I was like, "Um, yes."

The movie started at midnight down at the Village Cinema—about fifty blocks away. If I hurried, I could make it. Well, Lars and I could make it.

There was only one problem. We had no costumes: On Halloween, they don't let you into the theater if you come in street clothes.

"What do you mean, you don't have a costume?" Martha Stewart had overheard our conversation.

I held out the skirt of my dress. "Well," I said, dubiously. "I guess I could pass for Glinda the Good Witch. Only I don't have a wand. No crown, either."

I don't know if Martha had too many champagne cocktails, or if she's just like this, but next thing I knew, she was

whipping me up a wand from a bunch of crystal drink stir-
rers that she tied together with some ivy from the center-
piece. Then she fashioned this big crown for me out of some
menus and a glue gun she had in her purse.

And you know what? It looked good, just like the one in
The Wizard of Oz! (She turned the writing so it was on the
inside of the crown.)

"There," Martha said, when she was through. "Glinda
the Good Witch." She looked at Lars. "And you're easy.
You're James Bond."

Lars seemed pleased. You could tell he'd always fanta-
sized about being a secret agent.

No one was more pleased than me, however. My fantasy
of Michael seeing me in this gorgeous dress was about to
be realized. What's more, the outfit was going to give me
the confidence I needed to confront him about Jo-C-rox.

So, with my father's blessings—I would have stopped to
say good-bye to Grandmère, only she and Gerald Ford were
doing the tango out on the dance floor (no, I am not kidding)—I was out of there like a shot—

And stumbled right into a thorny patch of reporters.

"Princess Mia!" they yelled. "Princess Mia, what are
your feelings about your mother's elopement?"

I was about to let Lars hustle me into the limo without
saying anything to the reporters. But then I had an idea. I
grabbed the nearest microphone and said, "I just want to
say to anyone who is watching that Albert Einstein High
School is the best school in Manhattan, maybe even North
America, and that we have the most excellent faculty and
the best student population in the world, and anyone who

doesn't recognize that is just kidding himself, Mr. Taylor."

(Mr. Taylor is Shameeka's dad.)

Then I shoved the microphone back at its owner, and hopped into the limo.

We almost didn't make it. First of all, because of the parade, the traffic downtown was criminal. Secondly, there was a line to get into the Village Cinema that wound all the way around the block! I had the limo driver cruise the length of it, while Lars and I scanned the assorted hordes. It was pretty hard to recognize my friends, because everyone was in costume.

But then I saw this group of really weird-looking people dressed in WWII Army fatigues. They were all covered in fake blood, and some of them had phony stumps in place of limbs. They were holding a big sign that said *Looking for Private Ryan*. Standing next to them was a girl wearing a black lacy slip and a fake beard. And standing next to her was a boy dressed as a Mafioso type, holding a violin case.

The violin case was what did it.

"Stop the car!" I shrieked.

The limo pulled over, and Lars and I got out. The girl in the nightie went, "Oh, my God! You came! You came!"

It was Lilly. And standing next to her, a big pile of bloody intestines coming out of his Army jacket, was her brother, Michael.

"Quick," he said, to Lars and me. "Get in line. I got two extra tickets just in case you ended up making it after all."

There was some grumbling from the people behind us as Lars and I cut in, but all he had to do was turn so that his shoulder holster showed, and they got quiet pretty quick.

Lars's Glock, being real and all, was pretty scary-looking.

"Where's Hank?" Lilly wanted to know.

"He couldn't make it," I said. I didn't want to tell her why. You know, that last time I'd seen him, he'd been dancing with Gisele. I didn't want Lilly to think Hank preferred supermodels to, you know, us.

"He cannot come. Good," Boris said, firmly.

Lilly shot him a warning look, then, pointing at me, demanded, "What are you supposed to be?"

"Duh," I said. "I'm Glinda the Good Witch."

"I knew that," Michael said. "You look really . . . You look really . . ."

He seemed unable to go on. I must, I realized, with a sinking heart, look really stupid.

"You are way too glam for Halloween," Lilly declared.

Glam? Well, glam was better than stupid, I guess. But why couldn't Michael have said so?

I eyed her. "Um," I said. "What, exactly, are you?"

She fingered the straps to her slip, then fluffed out her fake beard.

"Hello," she said, in a very sarcastic voice. "I'm a Freudian slip."

Boris indicated his violin case. "And I am Al Capone," he said. "Chicago gangster."

"Good for you, Boris," I said, noticing he was wearing a sweater, and yes, it was tucked into his pants. He can't help being totally foreign, I guess.

Someone tugged on my skirt. I looked around, and there was Kenny, my Bio partner. He was in Army fatigues, too, and missing an arm.

"You made it!" he cried.

"I did," I said. The excitement in the air was contagious.

Then the line started moving. Michael and Kenny's friends from the Computer Club, who made up the rest of the bloody platoon, started marching and going, "Hut, two, three, four. Hut, two, three, four."

Well, they can't help it. They're in the computer club, after all.

It wasn't until the movie started that I began to realize something weird was going on. I very cleverly maneuvered myself in the aisle so that I would end up sitting next to Michael. Lars was supposed to be on my other side.

But somehow Lars got pushed out, and Kenny ended up on my other side.

Not that it mattered . . . then. Lars just sat behind me. I hardly noticed Kenny, even though he kept trying to talk to me, mostly about Bio. I answered him, but all I could think about was Michael. Did he really think I looked stupid? When should I mention that I happen to know that he is Jo-C-rox? I had this little speech all rehearsed. I was going to be like, Hey, seen any good cartoons lately?

Lame, I know, but how else was I supposed to bring it up?

I could hardly wait for the movie to be over so I could spring my offensive.

Rocky Horror, even if you can't wait for it to end, is pretty fun. Everybody just acts like a lunatic. People were throwing bread at the screen, and putting up umbrellas when it rained in the movie, and dancing the Pelvic Thrust. It really is one of the best movies of all time. It almost beats out

Dirty Dancing as my favorite, except, of course, there's no Patrick Swayze.

Except I forgot there aren't really any scary parts. So I didn't actually get a chance to pretend to be scared so Michael could put his arm around me, or anything.

Which kind of sucks, if you think about it.

But hey, I got to sit by him, didn't I? For like two hours. In the dark. That's something, isn't it? And he kept laughing and looking at me to see whether or not I was laughing, too. That counts, right? I mean, when someone keeps checking to see whether you think the same things are funny that he does? That totally counts for something.

The only problem was, I couldn't help noticing that Kenny was doing the same thing. You know, laughing and then looking at me to see if I was laughing, too.

That should have been my next clue.

After the movie, we all went out to breakfast at Round the Clock. And this is where things got even more weird.

I had been to Round the Clock before, of course—where else in Manhattan can you get pancakes for two dollars?—but never quite this late, and never with a bodyguard. Poor Lars was looking a little worse for wear by that time. He kept ordering cup after cup of coffee. I was jammed in at this table between Michael and Kenny—funny how that kept happening—with Lilly and Boris and the entire Computer Club all around us. Everyone was talking really loud and at the same time, and I was having a really hard time figuring out how I was ever going to bring up the cartoon thing, when all of a sudden, Kenny said, right in my ear, "Had any interesting mail lately?"

I am sorry to say that it was only then that the truth dawned.

I should have known, of course.

It hadn't been Michael. *Michael wasn't Jo-C-rox.*

I think a part of me must have known that all along. I mean, it really isn't like Michael to do anything anonymously. He just isn't the type not to sign his name. I guess I'd been suffering from a bad case of wishful thinking, or something.

A REALLY bad case of wishful thinking.

Because of course Jo-C-rox was Kenny.

Not that there's anything wrong with Kenny. There totally isn't. He is a really, really nice guy. I mean, I really like Kenny Showalter. Really, I do.

But he's not Michael Moscovitz.

I looked up at Kenny after he'd made that comment about having any interesting mail lately, and I tried to smile. I really did.

I said, "Oh, Kenny. Are you Jo-C-rox?"

Kenny grinned.

"Yes," Kenny said. "Didn't you figure it out?"

No. Because I am a complete idiot.

"Uh-huh," I said, forcing another smile. "Finally."

"Good." Kenny looked pleased. "Because you really do remind me of Josie, you know. Of *Josie and the Pussycats*, I mean. See, she's lead singer in a rock group, and she solves mysteries on the side. She's cool. Like you."

Oh, my God. *Kenny*. My Bio partner, *Kenny*. Six-foot-tall, totally gawky Kenny, who always gives me the answers in Bio. I'd forgotten he's like this huge Japanese anime fan.

Of course he watches the Cartoon Network. He's practically addicted to it. *Batman* is like his favorite thing of all time.

Oh, someone shoot me. Someone please shoot me.

I smiled. I'm afraid my smile was very weak.

But Kenny didn't care.

"And you know, in later episodes," Kenny said, encouraged by my smile, "Josie and the Pussycats go up into space. So she's also a pioneer into space exploration."

Oh, God, make this be a bad dream. Please make this be a bad dream, and let me wake up and have it not be true!

All I could do was thank my lucky stars that I hadn't said anything to Michael. Could you imagine if I'd gone up to him and said what I'd planned to? He'd have thought I'd forgotten to take my medication, or something.

"Anyway," Kenny said. "You want to go out sometime, Mia? With me, I mean?"

Oh, God. I hate that. I really hate that. You know, when people go "Do you want to go out with me sometime?" instead of "Do you want to go out with me next Tuesday?" Because that way you can make up an excuse. Because then you can always go, "Oh, no, on Tuesday I have this thing."

But you can't go, "No, I don't want to go out with you EVER."

Because that would be too mean.

And I can't be mean to Kenny. I like Kenny. I really do. He's very funny and sweet and everything.

But do I want his tongue in my mouth?

Not so much.

What could I say? "No, Kenny? No, Kenny, I don't want

to go out with you ever, because I happen to be in love with my best friend's brother?"

You can't say that.

Well, maybe some girls can.

But not me.

"Sure, Kenny," I said.

After all, how bad could a date with Kenny be? What doesn't kill us makes us stronger. That's what Grandmère says, anyway.

After that, I had no choice but to let Kenny put his arm around me—the only one he had, the other being tightly secured beneath his costume to give him the appearance of having been severely injured in a land mine explosion.

But we were all jammed in so closely at that table that Kenny's arm, as it went around my shoulders, jostled Michael, and he looked over at us. . . .

And then he looked over at Lars, really fast. Almost like he—I don't know . . .

Saw what was going on, and wanted Lars to put a stop to it?

No. No, of course not. It couldn't be that.

But it is true that when Lars, who was busy pouring sugar into like his fifth cup of coffee that night, didn't look up, Michael stood and said, "Well, I'm beat. What do you say we call it a night?"

Everyone looked at him like he was crazy. I mean, some people were still finishing their food and all. Lilly even went, "What's with you, Michael? Gotta catch up on your beauty sleep?"

But Michael totally took out his wallet and started counting out how much he owed.

So then I stood up really fast and said, "I'm tired, too. Lars, could you call the car?"

Lars, delighted finally to be leaving, whipped out his cell phone and started dialing. Kenny, beside me, started saying stuff like, "It's a shame you have to go so early," and "So, Mia, can I call you?"

This last question caused Lilly to look from me to Kenny and then back again. Then she looked at Michael. Then she stood up, too.

"Come on, Al," she said, giving Boris a tap on the head. "Let's blow this juke joint."

Only of course Boris didn't understand. "What is a juke joint?" he asked. "And why are we blowing it?"

Everyone started digging around for money to pay the bill . . . which was when I remembered that I didn't have any. Money, I mean. I didn't even have a purse to put money in. That was the one part of my wedding ensemble Grandmère had forgotten.

I elbowed Lars and whispered, "Have you got any cash? I'm a little low at the moment."

Lars nodded and reached for his wallet. That's when Kenny, who noticed this, went, "Oh, no, Mia. Your pancakes are on me."

This, of course, completely freaked me out. I didn't want Kenny to pay for my pancakes. Or Lars's five cups of coffee, either.

"Oh, no," I said. "That isn't necessary."

Which didn't have at all the desired effect, since Kenny said, all stiffly, "I insist," and started throwing dollar bills down on the table.

Remembering I'm supposed to be gracious, being a princess and all, I said, "Well, thank you very much, Kenny."

Which was when Lars handed Michael a twenty and said, "For the movie tickets."

Only then Michael wouldn't take my money—okay, it was Lars's money, but my dad totally would have paid him back—either. He looked totally embarrassed, and went, "Oh, no. My treat," even after I strenuously insisted.

So then I had to say, "Well, thank you very much, Michael," when all I really wanted to say was, "Get me out of here!"

Because with two different guys paying for me, it was like I'd been out on a date with both of them at once!

Which, I guess, in a way, I had.

You would think I would be very excited about this. I mean, considering I'd never really been out even with *one* guy before, let alone *two* at the same time.

Except that it was totally and completely *not* fun. Because, for one thing, I didn't actually want to be going out with one of them at all.

And for another, he was the one who'd actually confessed to liking me . . . even if it had been anonymous.

The whole thing was excruciating, and all I wanted to do was go home and get in bed and pull the covers up over my head and pretend it hadn't happened.

Only I couldn't even do that because, what with my mom and Mr. G being in Cancun, I had to stay up at the Plaza with Grandmère and my dad until they got back.

But just when I thought things had sunk to an all-time low, as everyone was piling into the limo (well, a few people asked for rides home, and how could I say no? It wasn't like we didn't have the room) Michael, who ended up standing beside me, waiting for his turn to get into the car, said, "What I meant to say before, Mia, was that you look . . . you look really . . ."

I blinked up at him in the pink-and-blue light from the neon Round the Clock sign in the window behind us. It's amazing, but even bathed in pink-and-blue neon, with fake intestines hanging out of his shirt, Michael still looked totally—

"You look really nice in that dress," he said, all in a rush.

I smiled up at him, feeling just like Cinderella all of a sudden. . . . You know, at the end of the Disney movie, when Prince Charming finally finds her and puts the slipper on her foot and her rags change back into the ball gown and all the mice come out and start singing?

That's how I felt, just for a second.

Then this voice right beside us said, "Are you guys coming, or what?" and we looked over and there was Kenny sticking his head and his one unsevered arm out of the sun roof of the limo.

"Um," I said, feeling totally and utterly embarrassed. "Yes."

And I got into the limo like nothing had happened.

And actually, if you think about it, nothing really had.

Except that the whole way back to the Plaza, this little voice inside my brain was going, "Michael said I looked nice. Michael said *I* looked nice. *Michael* said I looked nice."

And you know what? Maybe Michael didn't write those notes. And maybe he doesn't think I'm the Josiest girl in school.

But he thought I looked nice in my pink dress. And that's all that matters to me.

And now I am sitting in Grandmère's suite at the hotel, surrounded by piles of wedding and baby presents, with Rommel trembling down at the other end of the couch in a pink cashmere sweater. I am supposed to be writing thank-you notes, but of course I am writing in my journal instead.

No one seems to have noticed, though, I guess because Mamaw and Papaw are here. They stopped by to say good-bye on their way to the airport before they fly back to Indiana. Right now, my two grandmothers are making lists of baby names and talking about who to invite to the christening (oh, no. Not again.) while my dad and Papaw are talking about crop rotation, as this is an important topic to both Indiana farmers and Genovian olive growers. Even though, of course, Papaw owns a hardware store and Dad is a prince. But whatever. At least they're *talking*.

Hank is here, too, to say good-bye and to try to convince his grandparents they are not doing the wrong thing, leaving him here in New York—though to tell the truth, he isn't doing such a good job of it, since he hasn't once gotten off his cell phone since he arrived. Most of these calls seem to be from last night's bridesmaids.

And I'm thinking that, all in all, things aren't so bad. I mean, I am getting a baby brother or sister and have also acquired not just a stepfather who is exceptionally good at

Algebra, but a foozball table as well.

And my dad proved that there is at least one person on this planet who is not afraid of Grandmère . . . and even Grandmère seems a bit more mellow than usual, in spite of never having made it to Baden-Baden.

Though she still isn't talking to my dad, except when she absolutely has to.

And yes, it is true that later today I have to meet Kenny back at the Village Cinema for a Japanese anime marathon, since I said I would, and all.

But after that I am going down to Lilly's, and we are going to work on next week's show, which is about repressed memories. We are going to try to hypnotize each other and see if we can remember any of our past lives. Lilly is convinced, for instance, that in one of her past lives she was Elizabeth I.

You know what? I, for one, believe her.

Anyway, after that, I am spending the night at Lilly's, and we are going to rent *Dirty Dancing* and *Rocky Horror*-ize it. We plan to yell things in response to the actors' lines and throw things at the screen.

And there is a very good chance that tomorrow morning, Michael will come to the Moscovitzes' breakfast table wearing pajama bottoms and a robe, and forget to tie the robe like he did once before.

Which would actually make for a very profound moment, if you ask me.

A *very* profound moment.